The Case of the
Absent Author

The Case of the Absent Author

A McGURK MYSTERY

by E. W. HILDICK

Macmillan Books for Young Readers • New York

Macmillan Books for Young Readers
An imprint of Simon & Schuster Children's Publishing Division

Simon & Schuster Macmillan
1230 Avenue of the Americas
New York, New York 10020

Designed by Cathy Bobak
The text of this book is set in 12 point Caledonia.
Manufactured in U.S.A.
10 9 8 7 6 5 4 3 2 1

LIBRARY OF CONGRESS CATALOGING-IN-PUBLICATION DATA
Hildick, E. W. (Edmund Wallace), nd.
The case of the absent author : a McGurk mystery / by E. W. Hildick.
       p.   cm.
Summary: The six members of the McGurk Detective Organization, young amateur
detectives, are called on to help solve a case involving the disappearance of a
reclusive mystery writer.
ISBN 0-02-743821-X
[1. Mystery and detective stories.]   I. Title.
PZ7.H5463Caj   1995
[Fic]—dc20   94-26204

Contents

The Case of the
Absent Author

• 1 •

Buried Treasure?

I was working on my own that morning in McGurk's basement, headquarters of the McGurk Organization. It was during the summer vacation, and it was pouring rain. McGurk and the others were out on a training session—field training in judging walking distances. Someone had given him a pedometer, and he couldn't rest until he'd put it to use.

"Good *detective* use," he'd said.

I'd been excused—sprained ankle. It was practically mended, but I felt I'd be putting my time to better detective use by sorting out my files. They'd been getting untidy. I am the Organization's word expert and keeper of the records.

1

Anyway, there I was, sitting in McGurk's rocking chair, with the cardboard boxes labeled CASES SOLVED filling the whole table. Then came a knock at the outside door—the one five steps down from the backyard. I couldn't see who it was because of our sign taped to the glass panel. The sign is about three feet long, we've added so many things to it—like MYSTERIES SOLVED, and some weird ones like MUMMIES IMMOBILIZED.

I went across and opened up. It was a little guy in a gray business suit. He was carrying a leather document folder. He peered at me through purple-tinted glasses.

"Hello!" he said. "Are you Jack P. McGurk?"

"No," I said. "I'm Joey Rockaway."

"Oh . . ." He looked disappointed.

It was an understandable mistake. He must have peeked in around the corner of the sign and seen me sitting in the big chair—looking kind of distinguished, wearing large, businesslike glasses.

"This *is* where the McGurk Organization hangs out, though?"

"Yes," I said, letting him step in out of the rain. "I'm the Organization's record keeper and word expert. You can talk to me."

"Hmm! Where *is* McGurk?"

"Out on a field exercise with the others."

The man unzipped the folder and drew out a sheet of paper.

"The others, yeah . . ." He glanced at the paper. "If you're Joey Rockaway, that would leave . . . uh . . . Willie Sandusky, Wanda—"

"That's Willie Sand*ow*sky, sir," I corrected him. "Our smells expert."

"Your *what*?"

"He has this long, sensitive nose. Like a human blood-hound."

"Are you putting me on?" the newcomer growled.

"No, sir. He really can—"

"Okay, okay!" He glanced at the list again. "Then there's a coupla girls, right?"

"Yes, sir. There's Mari Yoshimura. She's Japanese. Our voice expert. She can do anything with her voice. Throw it. Imitate other people's voices . . ."

I reckon I'd started giving him a sales pitch. It looked like we might cop a handsome fee. But what would someone like that come to *us* for?

"Was there something you'd like us to—"

He waved me quiet. "And the other girl's called Wanda Grieg, yes?"

"Yes, sir. She's great at climbing. Especially trees."

"Really?" he said. "That could be very helpful in my case."

3

"Do you wish to discuss it, sir?" I said, pulling out one of the straight-backed chairs.

"Yes." He sat down. "But later. With McGurk himself. I only deal with principals."

"Principals?"

"Yes. The main men. The top honchos . . . I thought you said you were the word expert?"

"I am. But—"

"So what other experts does the McGurk Organization have? Besides sniffers, tree climbers, voice throwers, word slingers?"

"There's Brains Bellingham. Real name Gerald Bellingham. He's our science expert and—"

"Hold it!" He was looking very tense all at once. "*Gerald* Bellingham, you say? That would make his initials *G. B.* Hmm . . ." He seemed to relax. "A forensic guy, huh? Any more?"

"No. Just McGurk."

"Ah, the boss. What's *he* good at?"

Well, what could I tell him? Slave driving? Squeezing the last drop of energy from his team?

I thought it wiser not to mention any of that.

"Hunches," I said. "He has brilliant hunches."

"Terrific!" said the visitor. "The honcho with the hunches. Sounds like just my kind of guy."

Suddenly he looked toward the door.

Shadows. Voices.

"Ah, Jack McGurk!" he said as the door burst open. "We were just talking about you."

Brains stared at him through the rain beads on his glasses and blushed to the roots of his short, fair, bristly hair.

"No, sir!" he gasped. "That's McGurk up on the top step. The one with the red hair and freckles, doing all the talking."

That's just what McGurk *was* doing, saying, "You're all going to have to do better than *that*! Some of you can't even tell the difference between one hundred feet and half a mile!"

"I like him, I like him!" the visitor murmured. "He's got the right attitude. . . . Hi, McGurk! Glad to meet ya!"

McGurk looked startled. "Oh—uh—I didn't know . . . ," he mumbled, unclipping the pedometer from his belt. "I—uh—"

"The gentleman has a problem for us," I explained.

"Is that so?" McGurk suddenly brightened up. He took off his coat and shook it. "What's on your mind, sir?"

Then he frowned at me and reclaimed his rocking chair.

"Well . . . ," said the man doubtfully, looking at the

others—four soggy bundles, still in their outdoor clothes.

"That's okay, sir," said McGurk. "My officers have my complete confidence."

"Yes, well," the man continued, "it concerns an old friend of yours." He glanced at the damp newcomers. "And I'm glad to see you aren't put off by rain. There's gonna be plenty of outdoor legwork involved."

"Oh, boy!" groaned the dripping Wanda.

Even McGurk didn't look any too enthusiastic, until the man went on, "What it amounts to really, I guess, is a matter of buried treasure."

Suddenly everything went still.

McGurk stopped rocking.

Brains left off wiping his glasses with a dry piece of shirt.

Wanda quit fingering the damp tails of her long yellow hair.

Willie stopped sniffling.

Mari froze, one arm still in the sleeve of her raincoat.

"Jewels and stuff?" gasped Willie.

"Something every bit as valuable," said the man.

·2·

The Missing Mystery Writer

First things first," said McGurk. "Who *is* this old friend of ours?"

"You probably know him as Bill Smith," said the man.

We looked at one another. Six blank faces.

The visitor frowned. "Don't tell me he told you his *pen* name?"

"An *author*?" I gasped.

"Yeah . . ." The man took a deep breath. "Bill Legrand. I'm his agent. Sheldon Byrne. Here's my card." He passed it to McGurk.

"Bill Legrand, the great *crime writer*?" I said. "The author of the Lieutenant Carmichael books and TV series? About a New York police precinct?"

7

"Yeah," said Mr. Byrne. "With another twenty-six episodes coming up in the fall. Prime time."

Now McGurk was looking impressed. That show had given him some of his best ideas for running the Organization. Also, he'd nearly overdosed on fresh orange juice, the lieutenant's favorite drink.

"And doesn't he write the Felicity Snell mysteries, too?" asked Wanda. "About this small-town librarian who's so much smarter at solving crimes than the regular police?"

"Those, too," said Mr. Byrne. "With a major TV series planned for next year."

"Well!" said Wanda. "My mom reads them all the time. Wait till I tell her!"

"You'll do no such thing, young woman!" snapped the man. "Bill's secret must be respected at all times!"

"You bet, sir," said McGurk. "I'm surprised at you, Officer Grieg!"

"And don't forget the Mike Parker, Private Investigator books," Brains suddenly piped up.

"Right!" said the agent. "He writes them, too. . . . Uh . . . have *you* read any?"

Brains blushed again. "My uncle Jack left one lying around once. A paperback. About a killer who pickled his victims' livers in malt vinegar."

"That would be *Death in a Downtown Deli*," said Mr.

Byrne. "The Parker P.I. books are *very* popular."

"My mom took it away from me," said Brains. "Too adult. I only wanted to check if he'd gotten his medical facts right."

McGurk's green eyes gleamed as he turned to Mr. Byrne. "You said he was an old friend of *ours,* sir?"

"Well, an old acquaintance," said the man. "He just had to be. For him to get to know so much about you all."

"So much—?"

"Yeah. To put you in his last book. A Mike Parker. *The Apostle Killings.*"

McGurk glowed. "Us? In a book? A *private eye* book?"

"Yes, but don't get too excited. He didn't use your real names."

"What did he call *me,* then?" asked McGurk.

"Mac-something-or-other. I forget. The other kids called him Red." Mr. Byrne glanced at Willie's nose. "He called *him* Beaky. Oh, yeah, and the scientific one—he got called the Professor."

"The Professor?" murmured Wanda. "And Beaky? I seem to remember someone else calling them that once."

"Oh, I often get called the Professor," said Brains.

"So do I," I said. "I guess it's our glasses."

9

"How did we make out, sir?" said McGurk. "In the book. Did we help Mike Parker solve the case?"

"Well, not exactly," said Mr. Byrne. "You only come in as victims. A bunch of meddling amateurs who stumble onto a vital clue. The murderer has to rub them out—all six—uh . . . correction. Make that five. The Chinese girl was on vacation, luckily for *her*."

"Chinese, sir?" said Mari, looking slightly miffed.

"Yeah. Anna Chan. That's how he'd written *you* in, honey."

"Hmm!" murmured Mari.

None of this seemed to upset McGurk any. He was obviously still dazzled at the thought of being in a book.

Then he remembered the basic problem. "But how would Mr. Legrand know *us,* sir?"

"Well, the guy *lives* around here. That is, he does most of his writing here. Only a couple of miles away. In a cabin he rents over by the Old Post Road. In the woods."

"*I* didn't know Bill Legrand lived there," I said.

"Well, you should have, Officer Rockaway!" growled McGurk. "Being the word expert!"

"No, no!" said Mr. Byrne. "He *wouldn't* know. Bill always kept himself strictly anonymous. So he'd be left alone. He was a notorious recluse."

"Recluse?" said McGurk.

"A hermit," I explained.

"And a hermit who gave me a hard time!" grumbled the agent. "He'd never give television interviews or turn up for book signings. He wouldn't even supply clear pictures of himself for his book jackets. So now that he's gone missing again, we don't even have a decent photo to circulate!"

"Missing, sir?"

Mr. Byrne seemed too steamed up to hear Mari's question. "Mind you, being so retiring turned out to be good publicity in itself. The mystery-man element. Pure gold. Even so . . ." He shook his head.

"The treasure you mentioned, sir," said McGurk. "Is *that* gold? Did Mr. Le—uh—Smith bury it someplace? Before he went missing? And *when* did he go missing? And why did you say 'missing again'?"

Mr. Byrne sat back, looking more relaxed. "I see I've come to the right place, after all. You don't miss a trick, do you, McGurk? . . . Well, to answer your questions . . . One: No, it wasn't gold he buried. Two: He went missing over six weeks ago. And three: I said missing *again* because this isn't the first time." He sighed. "But it sure is the longest."

We all kept silent for a while.

Then McGurk spoke up. "You think something . . . something might have happened to him?"

The man sighed again. "Well, I'm not sure. When Bill takes it into his head to get into that old VW of his and go backpacking in some wilderness, he never leaves a forwarding address."

"Have you informed the police?" I asked.

"Uh-uh! Bill would never forgive me if the newspeople got hold of it, with all the publicity *that* would mean. . . . He'll *probably* turn up."

I noticed he'd crossed his fingers.

"So what's this buried treasure about?" said McGurk. "If it isn't gold or jewelry?"

· 3 ·

"Lambs to the Slaughter"

Manuscripts," Mr. Byrne said at last. "Books not yet published. New Felicity Snells. New Mike Parkers. New Lieutenant Carmichaels."

"But—"

"You see, Bill's such a fast worker," Mr. Byrne went on. "He writes eight or nine books a year. But he only publishes four. Which means he always has a stash in reserve."

"Like saving them up for a rainy day," murmured Wanda, fingering her wet hair.

"Yes," said Mr. Byrne. "So even if he went missing for keeps, there'd be a steady flow of Bill Legrand books for

13

years. Worth—well, with movie and TV rights—several million dollars."

"Wow!" gasped Willie.

"Yeah!" grunted the agent. "And now that rainy day's come. Nearly time for a new Felicity Snell to be sent to the publishers. Trouble is, Bill wasted the whole winter and spring on research for what he calls his Major Work."

"Oh?" I said.

"A huge blockbuster of a thing, yeah! Thinks it'll get him a Pulitzer Prize. All about crime in a medium-size American city like this. Every type of criminal you can think of. Petty crooks, big-time bosses, muggers, con artists, car thieves . . ."

"*We* might be able to help him with that, sir!" said McGurk.

"Don't *you* start getting big ideas!" said Mr. Byrne.

That was pretty much like asking a cat not to start hunting mice, but McGurk fell silent.

Mr. Byrne continued. "We were going to have to dip into Bill's stash for the new Felicity Snell. But—no stash in sight. And no Bill to ask where he hid it."

"Didn't he leave any instructions?" I asked.

"No. No *direct* ones, anyway."

McGurk pounced. "Some *clue* then?"

"Well, knowing the way Bill's mind works, there just has to be. That's why I thought he might have let something slip to you."

"But we never even *met* him, sir!" said McGurk.

"Maybe not so you'd notice," said Mr. Byrne. "But he certainly knew *you* guys, the way he wrote about those kids in *The Apostle Killings*. Also judging from *these*, which I found in his working notes." He pulled a sheaf of papers from his folder.

They proved to be newspaper clippings from our local daily, the *Gazette*. Plus this handwritten note pinned to the bunch:

Lambs to the Slaughter

McGurk didn't pay much attention to the note. He was more interested in reading—or rereading—the top clipping. Here's a copy:

YOUNG SLEUTHS DO IT AGAIN

CAT-STEALING RING TRACKED DOWN TO COUNTRY HIDEOUT

The kids who call themselves the McGurk Organization scored another big hit this week. While seeking a friend's missing cat, they stumbled onto the headquarters of a gang of tristate cat thieves in a remote barn near Brackman Swamp.

"Valuable Parrot"

"We were also looking for a valuable parrot stolen from Mrs. Berg," said red-haired Jack P. McGurk, 12. "We rescued that, too." "That's why we've called it the Case of the Purloined Parrot," chimed in studiously bespectacled record keeper Joseph Rockaway, 12, who

(Continued on page 8.)

The continuation clipping came next, plus others referring to a few more cases we've handled, like the Case of the Wandering Weathervanes and the Case of the Muttering Mummy.

We had them all in our own files, so we didn't waste any more time reading through them. Instead, we focused our attention on the handwritten note.

" 'Lambs to the Slaughter'?" McGurk murmured.

"Yes," said Mr. Byrne. "One of the chapter headings

16

in *The Apostle Killings*—where Bill dealt with the kids who blundered onto the killer. Like you stumbled onto the cat thieves."

"We didn't *stumble* onto them," said McGurk. "We tracked them down as a result of very careful detective work."

"Whatever," said the man. "And here—since you're such smart detectives—take a look at this."

He held out a slip of paper with a fancy blue-and-gold heading and a scrawled list. This:

THE SHELDON BYRNE AGENCY
LITERARY & TALENT
FROM THE OFFICE OF THE CHAIRMAN:

6-pack
G.B.
Magazines
Library
Renew Membership

"It isn't the same handwriting," I said, glancing at the "Lambs" note.

"No," said Mr. Byrne. "That's because it's *mine*. I copied the list from one I found on the cabin's refrigerator. Probably the last thing he wrote before he left."

"It's just a shopping list," said Wanda, shrugging.

"Oh, yes?" said the man. "Well, let me ask you something that might stir up your ideas. What's the six-pack doing there? Bill wasn't a beer drinker."

"Cokes?" said Mari. "Or some other soft drink?"

"Uh-uh! He was strictly a straight bourbon man when he was writing his Mike Parkers, milk when he was thinking about Felicity Snell, and fresh orange juice for Lieutenant Carmichael. And how about the G. B.?"

"Ground bait?" said Willie. "Like for fishing?"

"Bill wouldn't kill a fly," said Mr. Byrne.

"Well, gingerbread?" I suggested.

"Next!" he growled.

McGurk was frowning. "How about Gillette blades?"

"When he wasn't growing a beard, Bill used an electric shaver."

Brains coughed politely. "It—it could stand for Gerald Bellingham, I guess. But—"

"You're tootin' darned right it could!" said Mr. Byrne. "I mean, *six*-pack. What are *you* guys but a bunch of six? Huh? That's one reason I came here. And when I realized one of you had those initials—why, it's obvious! He was pointing to *you*. Or *beckoning* you."

McGurk's frown had deepened. "But . . . why G. B., sir? Why not J. P. McG.?"

"How should I know? Maybe he thought the Professor here was the real brains behind the outfit."

Brains's smirk broadened into a grin of delight—until he saw the look McGurk was giving him.

"Anyway, think," said Mr. Byrne. "Can't you remember someone coming here, maybe asking you to handle some penny-ante case? A man aged about fifty?"

"Height, weight, hair color?" asked McGurk acidly.

"Oh, well, you know—just an average, ordinary-looking bozo."

"Anyone?" said McGurk, looking around, still sore. "An average, ordinary-looking—uh—bozo?"

We shook our heads.

"Oh, for Pete's sake!" Mr. Byrne jumped to his feet. "You're as dumb as that bunch in *The Apostle Killings*! The—the MacTaggart Bureau. I remember what he called them now." He paused at the door. "And if *you* remember—about when he might have visited you—give me a call. Then I might think again about hiring you!"

And with that he went out and slammed the door.

"Wow!" murmured Willie. "What got into *him*?"

"He sounded very disappointed," said Mari.

19

"Yes," said Wanda. "I guess he'd been pinning a lot of hope on our help."

"He'd probably have paid well for it, too," said Brains wistfully. "I bet that was *his* Cadillac parked outside."

"McGurk?" I said anxiously.

His head was bowed, his eyes were closed, his ears were burning.

"Officer Rockaway . . . ," he said in a small, still voice.

"Yes?"

"What's that song they sing at New Year's?"

"Uh . . . 'Should auld acquaintance be forgot . . . '?"

"Yeah," he grunted. "Well, now it looks like it'll have a new ending."

"Oh? What?"

"This!" he roared. " 'Should auld acquaintance be forgot, the McGurk Organization looks like it'll lose out on the chance of a very important case!'" He glared around. "Come on, *think*! Rack your brains! Reach into your memories! When could this Bill Smith have seen us here, in our own HQ? Who did he pretend to be? What was his excuse for getting this close?"

•4•

The Stringer

Well, we did all that.
 We thought.
We racked our brains.
We reached into our memories.
And we did this for a whole *hour.*
Some of us did it with our eyes closed or half closed and our heads sunk onto our chests. Willie was one of these.

Brains and Wanda stared up at the ceiling, as if that was where they stored their memories.

Mari went into a corner and muttered. She told me later that she was trying out all the voices she'd ever heard in our basement. The ones she focused on were people who'd come as clients, kids like Ray Williams and Sandra Ennis. The only men's voices that came back to her, though, were those of Wanda's brother Ed and our friend Patrolman Cassidy. And neither of *them* could have been Bill Legrand, a.k.a. Smith!

McGurk's memory bank was a mobile one. He prowled around that basement the whole time. Staring at the files, the copying machine, my typewriter, the door, the rug, us, everything. But nothing seemed to jog the memory he was reaching for. His freckles bunched up closer with every circuit, and his eyes seemed to get glassier and glassier.

Then Willie snored. There was no mistaking it. When Willie snores, he *snores*.

"Officer Sandowsky!" yelped McGurk.

I guess it had startled the rest of us out of our trances, too. Willie was looking terribly confused.

"You were *asleep*!" Wanda accused him.

"No, I . . . uh . . . I coughed—something in my throat—back of my nose . . ."

"How about something in back of your *memory*?" said McGurk. "How about keeping awake and alert for—" He broke off. "What is it, Officer Sandowsky?"

"I—I think I was kind of *hypnotized* just then!"

"Huh?"

"Yeah! I wasn't *asleep*. I was . . . well . . . It was you, McGurk, going around and around. And Mari mumbling away in the corner there. It had me feeling dizzy. And . . . and . . . I *did* remember something!"

"Oh?" McGurk grabbed him by the shoulders. "What? Huh? *What?*"

"It was one time in this basement. When there were visitors. Men. Strangers. Asking questions . . . Hey, McGurk! You're hurting my shoulders!"

McGurk released him in midshake. "*Who*, Officer Sandowsky? *What* questions?"

"When that guy from the *Gazette* came to interview us. Mark Westover. After the parrot case."

"Mark Westover isn't a stranger," I said. "And if *he* was the author of all those Bill Legrand books, *he* wouldn't be able to keep quiet about it!"

"And you couldn't call him ordinary-looking," said Wanda. "Not with *his* height."

"No," said McGurk, "but there was another reporter with him. It's coming back to me now. A guy from some other paper. Right, Officer Sandowsky?"

"Yeah. But I hope his *face* has come back to you, McGurk. All *I* get is a blank."

I could recall the occasion myself now, but the features of the second man were very vague. When Mark

Westover's around, asking all the questions, getting you to speak into his tape recorder, it kind of puts everyone else in the shade. Especially when you're busy wondering if he's going to get it right and not say you *stumbled* onto something when you'd really been working very hard.

The others looked just as uneasy—also remembering the occasion but not the details. Even McGurk was stumped.

"Who could be so ordinary-looking he's almost invisible?" Wanda grumbled.

"Bill Smith, that's who!" said McGurk. "I'd stake our reputation on it. It was a perfect opportunity for him to get to know all about us, while Mark Westover was doing the talking. All Bill Smith had to do was keep his ears and eyes open and make notes."

"So what do we do now?" I said.

"Meet up here with your bikes, straight after lunch," he replied. "Then we'll go to the *Gazette* office and see if Mark Westover remembers who that guy was. Or *said* he was!"

There was a rainbow over the *Gazette* building, but we didn't find much of a pot of gold there. Not at first.

Oh, sure—Mark Westover came to the front office quickly enough. He's had too many juicy stories from the McGurk Organization for him to give us the brush-off.

And sure—after he'd racked *his* brains, he said, "Ah, yes! I remember the guy now. I couldn't think for the moment, he's such a shadowy character. Haven't seen him around in months."

"What's his *name*?" McGurk asked eagerly.

I held my notebook poised, ready.

Mark Westover shrugged. "I can't remember. Something very *ordinary*. Just like him."

"Here we go again!" murmured Wanda.

"What paper did he work for?" asked McGurk.

"Oh, none in particular," said Mark. "He's a stringer."

"A what?"

"A guy who works freelance. Earns a few dollars picking up unusual local news items and selling them to larger papers elsewhere."

"Did he say which papers?" I asked.

"He might have. I've a feeling he mentioned some southern sheets. *Atlanta Constitution* . . . *Charlotte Observer* . . . what I do know is that he seemed interested mainly in crime. All kinds."

25

"Oh, yes?" said McGurk, suddenly alert.

"Yes. Especially unusual stuff. Like the kind you're always stumbling across."

"How did you get to know him?" McGurk asked patiently.

"It was more like *he* got to know *me*. I think it was in a diner. After that, he'd tag along occasionally when I was out on a story."

"Didn't you *mind*?" asked Wanda.

"No. It wasn't as if he worked for one of our rivals here. Besides"—Mark gave a dry, scornful laugh—"*he* was no threat, poor guy! *Way* over the hill."

"How's that?" said McGurk.

"Well, the way he was equipped. Didn't *you* notice, Joey?" I looked up at him. Like I said before, who'd notice anyone else when *he* was in the room, doing all the talking.

"No," I muttered, ignoring McGurk's "shame on you" glare.

"Well, he was using a cheap notebook like yours. And not even a ballpoint pen," the tall reporter added, eyeing mine. "Just a stub of lead pencil sharpened at both ends. Scribbling away in shorthand like a reporter in an old movie."

I wasn't using shorthand, but I wasn't doing so great in longhand, either. Here's all I'd got, up until then:

26

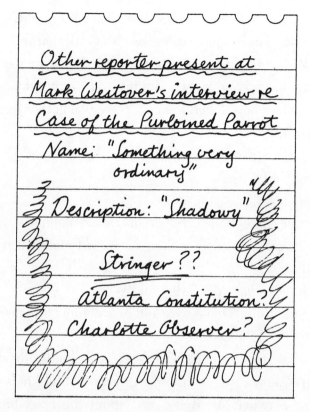

Other reporter present at
Mark Westover's interview re
Case of the Purloined Parrot

Name: "Something very
ordinary"

Description: "Shadowy"

Stringer ??

Atlanta Constitution?

Charlotte Observer?

The scribbles? Doodling. Thinking about how it was like trying to see someone in a cloud of thick smoke.

"Anyway, why so interested?" said Mark Westover.

"Oh, just wondering what he might have written about us," said McGurk.

"Getting around to it rather late, aren't you? That was over a year ago." The reporter's eyes narrowed suspiciously. "He hasn't turned up dead in some back alley, has he? He always seemed the kind who might."

"What kind is that, sir?" asked McGurk sharply.

"Well, you know—the kind who dies a mysterious death and no one knows who his relatives are, let alone who might have killed him. . . . *Have* you gotten wind of something?"

McGurk shook his head. "No . . . just curious. Thanks anyway, Mr. Westover."

Outside, though, he dropped his casual manner.

"Bingo!" he yelled, looking like *he'd* found that pot of gold.

"Bingo *what,* McGurk?" said Willie.

"Bill Smith! That—what did he call him? Stinger?"

"Stringer," I said.

"That stringer *must* have been Bill Smith. Someone who'd shown special interest in crime of all kinds. Remember what Mr. Byrne said about the book he was working on?"

"Yes," said Brains. "But it doesn't tell us much else. I don't remember that guy saying *anything* that time."

He had a point there. Even McGurk had to agree. But as we got back onto our bikes, he said, "Anyway, let's hope Bill Legrand *doesn't* turn up dead in some back alley . . . or in some *backwoods.* Come on, men. Let's go take a look at that cabin."

· 5 ·

The Cabin in the Woods

The burned-out motel on the Old Post Road had been the scene of one of our most hair-raising experiences. But as we cycled past, McGurk hardly glanced at it, with its bouncing bets growing among the rubble, waving at us as if to say, "Hey! Remember when you were kidnapped here by a criminal in a camper?"

"These must be the woods," he said, nodding across to our left.

The trees had NO HUNTING notices posted on their trunks every few yards. Blue flowers were growing at the edge of the woods, and when Mari admired them, Wanda told her they were chicory. "And these orange flowers are wood lilies."

"Marking the entrance to his driveway, I bet," said McGurk.

Well, they were *all* that marked it. There was no sign or gate or anything. And it was more like a lumber trail than a regular driveway—with rainwater gleaming in old tire tracks, and tufts of new grass growing between them.

"It hasn't been used much lately," said Brains.

"No," said McGurk. "This has to be the place, men. Come on."

We followed him. The leaves were still dripping after the last shower, and the tunnel-like track soon echoed with our yells as some of the splashes hit the backs of our necks.

"Cut it out!" growled McGurk. "Who knows what might be lurking along here?"

Well, that quieted us some. But the ruts didn't get any better, causing a few spills, with more yells and groans, before finally we came to a clearing. Then the groans became sighs of relief, because there, at last, was the cabin.

It was single-story, of course, with darkened cedar shingles. The windows were murky behind dirty screens. There was a rough stone chimney, and the whole building was based on a stone foundation. Like our HQ, it had five steps—but these led *up* to the door, not down. And:

"Hey! It's open!" said Willie.

"Mr. Byrne?" said Brains.

"What?" said Wanda. "Coming here on *foot*?"

There was what looked like a parking space near the log pile at the corner, but no car. Willie said, "Maybe Mr. *Smith* has come back."

"There goes our case if he has!" muttered McGurk.

"I suppose *you'd* prefer he *was* lying dead in a ditch!" said Wanda.

"I didn't say that," he retorted. "Anyway, *his* car isn't here, either. Didn't Mr. Byrne say something about an old VW? I—"

"*Freeze!*"

I felt my blood do just that as I turned. The speaker must have crept around the corner while we were staring at the door.

He was standing at the side of the log pile, peering at us along the twin barrels of a shotgun. He was wearing a light-blue sweatshirt and sweatpants, with very muddy running shoes. Then he lowered the gun slightly.

His face was that of an old man—bald, lean, brown— with a fringe of white hair.

"Heh-heh! Gotcha! I knew you'd be around some- place close."

"Sir?"

There could be no misunderstanding the innocence

31

in McGurk's voice. The man took a step forward, peered closer, then lowered his gun.

"Oh, all right. I didn't expect kids. Kids would normally have vandalized the place, I guess. Why didn't you?"

We still stared at him, perplexed.

"We've only just got here, sir," said McGurk.

"We saw the door was open," Wanda began, "and—"

"That's what I did," said the man. "Half an hour ago. I was just coming back from my afternoon jog, when *I* noticed the door ajar. So I hurried along to my house"—he nodded beyond the cabin to where the dirt road continued, rising into more trees—"for the gun. I didn't really expect to catch anyone, but you never know."

McGurk seemed about to say something, but the man was racing on: "Anyway, it seemed to be undisturbed when I went inside. And I was just thinking it must have been some vagrant who'd wandered in out of the rain, when I heard voices out here."

"And thought it was—?"

"So I tippy-toed out the back way, and here we are. My name's Logan. Craig Logan, *Esquire.* I own this land. I rent this cabin to folks who want peace and quiet. Who are *you*?"

I recognized him now, from his pictures in the *Gazette.* One of the wealthiest men in these parts. President of the country club and the chamber of commerce. He'd celebrated his eightieth birthday recently, which was when I'd seen his latest pictures.

McGurk began, "We're the McGurk Organization, sir. We . . . we investigate things."

"Investigate?" said Mr. Logan, giving him a piercing look. "Investigate what?"

"Uh—cases and stuff—"

I was embarrased for McGurk. Here he was—one principal talking to another principal—and all he could do was stammer about "cases and stuff"!

"Cases, huh?" Mr. Logan grunted. "I've handled more cases than you've had peanut-butter sandwiches."

"Were *you* a detective, sir?" McGurk said.

"A detective? Me? One of the leading attorneys-at-law in the state? Who just missed out on being the state's attorney general? I've employed detectives. I've hired them and fired them. I've eaten them for breakfast." His cheeks were glowing dusky red. "And what's with this '*were* you'? I still *am* a leading attorney-at-law. Over half a century at the bar—"

He broke off. At first I thought he must have spotted Mari's lips moving as she silently echoed his words. "What's *your* name?"

"Mari Yoshimura, sir."

"I *thought* so. You resemble your charming mother. Your father's a client of mine. My firm handles all his firm's legal business in the U.S." Leaving even Mari looking awed, he swung to Wanda. "And what are *you* staring at, young lady?"

"I—I was just thinking about your jogging, sir."

That seemed to delight him. "You mean at my time of life? Ha! I bet I could outrun any of *you*, even now!"

He laid the gun down on the log pile and looked as if he meant to challenge us all to a one-hundred-yard dash there and then.

"We really came to see if Mr. Le—uh, Smith was home, sir," McGurk said hurriedly.

The man stiffened. All the fun and the rather childish boastfulness left him, as if at the flip of a switch.

"Mr. Smith hasn't been here in weeks. Mr. Smith has vanished. Mr. Smith has left no forwarding address. . . . But then, he never does. Never has done. All the time he's been my tenant." Then he pounced. "But tell me this—and have a care how you answer. Why did you call him Mr. LeSmith? Eh? Hmm?"

McGurk blinked.

The gray eyes of Mr. Craig Logan, attorney-at-law, had suddenly become very hard and bright. Like the tips of a couple of tungsten drills.

McGurk swallowed. "Just—just a slip of the tongue, sir!"

·6·

The Voice of Bill Legrand

Then the attorney relaxed.

"Don't mind me, son," he said. "It's an old habit. Anyone stumbles over an answer, I pounce. Can't help it. Like a cat on a mouse. All those years in court. All those lying crooks. Two wives divorced me over that habit." He sighed. "So what did you wish to see the elusive Mr. Smith about? Hmm? Nothing urgent, I hope."

"His—uh—business partner asked us to investigate, sir," said McGurk. "He thought Mr. Smith might have left some kind of clue with us."

The man's eyes narrowed. "You knew him, then?"

"Slightly, sir."

"A clue about what?"

"About where he might have"—McGurk hesitated—"gone."

Mr. Logan checked himself in midpounce. "You said his business partner?"

"Yes, sir. Mr. Byrne."

"Oh, *him.* Yes, he was here yesterday afternoon." Mr. Logan frowned. "I suppose *he* could have left the door open."

"Have you reported this to the police, sir?" asked McGurk.

"But I've told you. Nothing seems to be missing. No damage, as far as—"

"No, sir," McGurk cut in. "I meant, have you reported Mr. Smith missing?"

"Oh, *that?*" Mr. Logan shook his head. "No. As I also told you, he's always coming and going without informing me. He—" A large blue Cadillac was cautiously entering the clearing. "Here's Mr. Byrne now."

As the little agent stopped the car and stepped out, he stared at us.

"Afternoon, Mr. Logan," he said briefly, still looking at us. "What are *you* guys doing here?"

"Looking for clues, sir," said McGurk.

"We've remembered—" Willie began, but Mr. Byrne checked him.

"Later . . . What's the door doing open?"

"We were just discussing that," said Mr. Logan. Then he told the agent about his encounter with us. "I thought at first it was they who'd been the intruders," he concluded.

"So who was it?" said Mr. Byrne.

"I've no idea. I suppose *you* couldn't have forgotten to close it properly yesterday?"

"Not a chance," said Mr. Byrne.

The other shrugged and picked up his gun. "Anyway, I'd better be moseying along."

When the old man was out of sight, Mr. Byrne turned to McGurk. "You didn't let anything slip, did you? About Bill Smith being Bill Legrand?"

"No, sir," said McGurk, reddening slightly.

"Or about the stash of manuscripts?"

"Of course not, sir."

"Good. *He* doesn't know Bill's secret. If he did, the old jackass would blabber it all over town." He turned to Willie. "You say you've remembered? You mean about Bill coming to see you? In your—uh—office?" By now he was addressing McGurk again.

"We think it might have been him," our leader said. Then he reported on our visit to Mark Westover.

"Did you tell *him* about Bill Legrand?" Mr. Byrne asked.

"No, sir."

"No; I guess he'd be here right now if you had." Mr. Byrne frowned thoughtfully. "Did Bill say much? The time he tagged along with Westover?"

"Hardly anything," I said. "Just made shorthand notes."

"Hmm!" murmured the agent. "He usually works with a tape recorder when he's doing research. In fact—"

"Maybe the notebook was part of his cover," said McGurk.

"Yes, well," said Mr. Byrne, "Bill did start his career as a cub reporter. Back in Charleston. He'd know what props to use. But as I said, he uses a tape recorder nowadays. Like this."

We stared at the small black object he'd taken from his document folder. It was flat and compact.

"Hey! A microcassette!" said Brains. "That's a state-of-the-art model!"

"I found it in his New York apartment," said Mr. Byrne. "It was in an envelope labeled 'Notes for the McGurk Organization'—"

"What?"

"Yeah. Probably in connection with *The Apostle Killings*. Only he'd wiped them out by recording some new notes."

"What are these new notes, sir?" asked McGurk.

"Not much. Merely about some books he was read-ing. Or intending to read."

"May we hear it, sir?" Mari asked. "For his voice?"

"Well, now you've made *some* progress, I guess I'll hire you after all." Mr. Byrne handed the recorder to McGurk. "Take it. It might help jog your memories some more." He glanced up at the sky. "But let's go in-side, huh?"

I don't think any of us were bothered by the sudden shower as we trooped into the cabin. We didn't even pay much attention to the place itself right then. All our at-tention was focused on the recorder as McGurk switched it on.

Here's the transcript I made later:

Transcript of notes recorded on tape by B.Smith a.k.a. B. Legrand

Voice: Get hold of copy of Poe's Tales of Mystery and Imagination and reread "The Black Cat." Excellent example of the criminal mind believing itself invincible.

(Pause # 1)

Also "The Purloined Letter" — masterpiece of detection. Plus the art of hiding something and searching for something hidden. Probably inspired the Sherlock Holmes stories.

(Pause # 2)

Also a copy of his poem "The Raven," and his essay "The Philosophy of Composition" for his description of how he came to write that poem. A masterpiece of reconstruction.

(Pause # 3)

N.B. Especially his reason for choosing a <u>raven</u> for his talking bird and not — uh — any other talking bird.

(Pause # 4)

END OF RECORDING

During the first pause there came the sound of a siren in the background.

In the second pause, we could hear other traffic noises.

The third pause was a light drumming sound. It was somehow very familiar. Mari identified it later as the drumming of fingers on a tabletop, with the speaker deep in thought.

In the final pause, before the click that marked the end, we heard someone laugh softly.

The speaker himself?

Or someone else with him?

And was it an innocent chuckle? Or an evil snigger?

We spent many hours later, wondering. Even Mari couldn't be certain. But she was sure of one thing.

"A southern voice," she murmured.

"Yes, Bill's," said Mr. Byrne. "He was raised in South Carolina."

"It was obviously recorded in a city apartment," said Brains. "Not here."

"Yes," said the agent. "His own, probably. East Sixty-eighth Street."

"Could he have stashed his manuscripts *there*?" asked McGurk.

"Don't think I haven't looked! But no. He very rarely used the apartment—only when he came to the city on business, or to do some research."

"Hey, yes!" I said. "Like at the New York Public Library."

Mr. Byrne smiled approvingly. "Your assistants aren't *totally* dumb, McGurk."

"No, sir," he said. "I train them well. But about the stash. You searched his apartment thoroughly?"

"Like I was looking for that purloined letter. And this stash ain't no letter. Most likely it's a large suitcase. No, son. It's here or somewhere around here that he's hidden it."

By now I was beginning to look around. We were in

the living room. A plain table, a fancy painted straight-backed chair, an overstuffed leather armchair, a shelf with a row of old books, and a mug bristling with pens and pencils. No television. A wide fireplace with charred logs. And dust all over, in a thick layer.

McGurk was looking around, too. Wanda was clucking over some withered flowers in a dried-out vase. And Willie—*he* had drifted off into another room, sniffing as he went.

Then he suddenly called out, "Hey! Here's the shopping list again!"

Well, we'd already gotten a copy, but we went in, anyway, eager to explore and show Mr. Byrne just how right he'd been in hiring us.

Willie was pointing at the memo board stuck with a magnet to the refrigerator door. Dangling from the board on a gilt chain was a felt pen filled with black erasable ink.

And here's a copy—an *accurate* copy—of that list:

6-pack
G-B
Magazines
Library
Renew membership

"Forget-me-nots," said Wanda, staring at the painted flowers.

"Officer Grieg," said McGurk, "we haven't come here on a nature walk." He turned to me. "And what are you looking so puzzled about? It's the same list as the client's copy."

He'd pulled it from his pocket. "Sure is!" said Mr. Byrne. "An *exact* copy."

"Well . . . 'exact' . . . ," I murmured, looking from the slip of paper to the board.

"I didn't draw the *flowers,* for Pete's sake!" said Mr. Byrne.

"No, sir," I said. "But there's *something* different. . . ."

"What?" McGurk asked sharply.

"I just can't put my finger on it. But—"

"And I didn't try to copy his handwriting, either," said Mr. Byrne. "What *is* this, Officer Word Expert? Did I spell something wrong? We principals pay secretaries to check that stuff. Right, McGurk?"

"Think, Officer Rockaway!" said McGurk, ignoring his fellow principal's question. (When it comes right down to it, McGurk knows the value of his officers' observations.)

"I tell you, I can't pinpoint it, McGurk, but there's something not quite right."

"Maybe it's his writing that's hurried," said Mr. Byrne.

43

"Yes, and talking of leaving in a hurry—" Wanda began, ready to throw the withered flowers into the kitchen trash can. "These—"

"Hold it!" said McGurk. "Any other garbage in there?"

"No," said Mr. Byrne. "The gunk inside was beginning to stink when I came to look around after he'd been gone a couple of weeks. So I took it out."

"Pity!" said McGurk. "You can sometimes pick up valuable clues from garbage."

(For some reason, a picture of the burned-out motel flashed through my mind.)

"Well, it told me that Bill *definitely* left in a hurry," said Mr. Byrne. "He usually empties the garbage and cleans out the refrigerator before he goes off on one of his trips."

"Oh, really?" said McGurk, reaching out to the refrigerator-door handle.

"Don't bother, McGurk," said Willie. "I already looked. It's empty."

"Yes, I saw to *that*, too," said Mr. Byrne. "Bill must have switched if off *ready* to clear it out. But I guess something happened that made him abandon the job. And—pow!—that was one powerful reek!"

"It sure would have been!" said Willie. "Tuna fish and

cottage cheese, mainly." He sniffed. "Oh, yes—plus half a grapefruit."

Mr. Byrne gaped at him. "How did you know *that*?"

"Officer Sandowsky has a very sensitive nose, sir," McGurk explained.

Willie wrinkled that nose. "You shoulda washed the shelves out."

"Hey! I'm the guy's agent!" yelped Mr. Byrne. "Not his *maid*!"

"Anyway, that's another clue," said McGurk. "He must have left in an even bigger hurry than I thought."

"Excuse *me*!" Wanda was sounding impatient. "These flowers"—she pitched them into the can—"they were probably the last he picked. Wood lilies and bouncing bets. I'd say they were six or seven weeks dead."

"So?" growled McGurk.

"So anyone who cares enough about wildflowers to pick them and take them indoors—he doesn't just leave them to wither in a vase. Not unless he's in a really *terrible* hurry."

"She might have something there, McGurk," said Mr. Byrne. "Bill did care for wildflowers. Enough to make himself a wildflower garden around the back."

McGurk turned back to the list. "I'm beginning to get a sense of what might have happened," he murmured.

"Oh?"

"Yeah. All this about leaving unexpectedly. It might explain the *G. B.*"

"How's that?" said Brains.

"Maybe he heard a car arriving," said McGurk. "Late at night. Maybe they'd come to kidnap him and he suddenly realized this. A car with British license plates—*G. B.* for Great Britain. Maybe he only had time to scribble those initials down!"

We stared. Willie was looking nervous. I mean, this was a very *lurid* picture of Bill Legrand's last night at home.

"Maybe," McGurk continued slowly, "it was his last evening *alive!*"

Even Mr. Byrne had fallen silent.

Then Mari let in a little real daylight. "So why aren't those initials at the *end* of the list, Chief McGurk?"

McGurk, who'd been scowling at them as if they'd been scrawled in the writer's blood, suddenly sighed. "I guess you have a point there, Officer Yoshimura."

"Anyway," said Mr. Byrne, a little sourly, "let me give you a tour of the cabin. See if any *more* bright ideas occur to you. . . ."

· 7 ·

And a Voice from the Grave!

The next room contained a single bed, a pinewood clothes closet, and a small chest of drawers. Mr. Byrne pulled out the drawers to show us the very few neatly folded clothes.

"It doesn't mean he'd taken most of his stuff with him," the agent said. "I mean, what would he have packed it in? He only ever used one suitcase and a backpack." He opened the clothes closet. "And they're in here still. Both empty. Probably he intended to buy a new outfit on the trip."

Sure enough, the brown tweed jacket hanging there looked ready to drop to bits. Likewise the old backpack, collapsed on the bottom, and the suitcase, together with a very ancient-looking typewriter.

That reminded me. "Where does he keep his word processor?"

"*This* was Bill's word processor," said Mr. Byrne.

We stared at the typewriter. Its bulky, silvery body was tarnished and chipped.

"It isn't even an *electric* model!" said Brains. "It's a stone-age Remington manual!"

"It must be more than thirty years old!" I said.

"Yes," said Mr. Byrne, grinning.

"You mean, Bill Legrand, author of all those books—?" McGurk began.

"Sure," said the agent. "He could have afforded a state-of-the-art word processor in every room. In fact, he only used *this* after he'd written a book in longhand first."

"Then the ones he's stashed—"

"Yeah. They really are manuscripts, not typescripts. As you'll see when—uh—*if* you track them down."

"I guess it makes sense," said Wanda. "That way, he'd still be able to write in the wilderness."

"You've got it, young lady. One of his best Mike Parkers was written in longhand somewhere in the Canadian Rockies. He couldn't very well carry a typewriter like this in his backpack. . . . But let's move on."

The bathroom was very small—just a toilet, a shower stall, and a sink.

"There's nothing much in *there*," the man said as McGurk reached up to the wall cabinet. "Just the usual stuff. You can go through that later. There's one more room I suppose I ought to show you. Down below. The root cellar."

He led the way back to the kitchen and took down a key hanging from a nail. Then we followed him into the backyard and down three or four steps like those leading to McGurk's basement.

But there the resemblance ended. The cellar was small and windowless. The only light came from the open door, so it was pretty dim in there. The walls were bare stone, mildewy and glistening in places, and the floor was plain concrete. There was no furnishing at all, not even a stone table or shelves. The air felt clammy.

"It reminds me of that story he mentioned on his tape recorder," I said.

"Which one?" said McGurk.

" 'The Black Cat.' Don't you remember? It was on 'Chiller Theater' not long ago. Where the guy murders his wife and bricks the corpse up behind the cellar wall."

"Go on," said McGurk, *very* alert now. "What else? He might have been pointing us to something."

"Yes," said Mr. Byrne. "*I* don't know the story, either."

49

"*I* remember it," said Wanda. "The murderer shows the police around to prove the missing woman isn't there. Getting overconfident, thinking he's committed the perfect crime."

"But overlooking one thing," I said. "While he was bricking the body up, he didn't notice his wife's favorite cat sneaking into the cavity."

"And just as the police are about to leave the cellar, satisfied," said Wanda, "the cat begins to squawl and yell behind the bricks and—"

"*Meeeow!*"

It seemed to come from the wall in front of us. And, boy, did that give us a scare! We were crowded close together, and the shock wave went tingling through us as if we were one body.

Well, *nearly* all of us.

"Officer Yoshimura!" McGurk suddenly growled.

"Sorry, Chief McGurk!" said Mari, hanging her head.

"She's an expert voice thrower," McGurk said on the way out. "She sometimes gets carried away."

"Huh!" exclaimed Mr. Byrne. "I nearly had a heart attack! Then *I'd* a got carried away!"

It sure *speeded* him on his way.

"Here," he said, handing McGurk the key to the cabin. "I'm leaving it with you. But only for daytime use. I don't want you holding any wild all-night parties."

50

"As if we *would*!" said Wanda.

"Yeah!" grunted Mr. Byrne, giving Mari an extremely cautious glance. "Anyway, I expect you to get right down to your job and not let up until you find those manuscripts."

"You can count on us, sir," said McGurk.

"Not that he'd stash them *inside* the cabin," Mr. Byrne continued. "Someplace that might catch fire and destroy them within minutes."

"No, sir. My guess is—"

"Let me finish, McGurk. . . . Knowing Bill, I'm pretty sure he'd choose somewhere fireproof."

"So—," McGurk began again.

"My *own* hunch," said Mr. Byrne, "is that the stash is buried someplace out there in the woods. Where no one's likely to go digging and find it accidentally. But exactly where in the woods—well, I still think he must have left a clue, in case anything happened to him. And a clue only a chosen person or bunch of persons would be able to recognize."

"*Us*," said our leader.

"Right, McGurk. You've remembered what I said about that six-pack. Which is why I'm counting on you." Mr. Byrne paused at the door. "Hey, and don't forget. Your mission is to track down the stash, not find out what happened to Bill. That could be more a matter for the police. If . . . uh . . . he hasn't just taken off for a longer trip than usual."

"We'll be careful, sir," said McGurk.

"Good," said Mr. Byrne. "You've got my office number. The minute you turn anything up, let me know. . . . I'll just stop by at old Logan's place and let him know I've given you the key."

After our client had gone, McGurk clapped his hands. "You heard what he said, men. Let's get on and— What are you doing, Officer Rockaway?"

"Oh . . . nothing." I'd picked up the mug of pens. "I was just wondering if he used a different pen for a different kind of story. This black one for a Mike Parker, the blue one for—"

"*Cut it out, Officer Rockaway!* That has nothing to do with the case! Focus your—" McGurk stared. "What *now?*"

I guess Mari's bricked-up cat had set my nerves on edge. McGurk's sudden angry outburst had made me jump, causing the mug in my left hand to rattle.

Which was strange, because I'd taken the pens out and was holding them in my right hand.

"Hey! Look at *this!*" I said, removing the object that I hadn't noticed until then.

It was a pencil stub, a couple of inches long.

And sharpened at both ends!

I made this note of it—*with* it, in fact—on the spot:

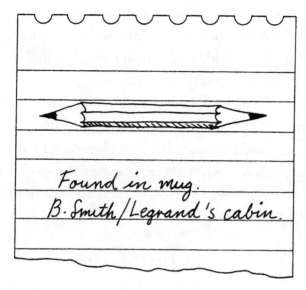

"Well that clinches it," said McGurk. "That really had to be Bill Smith who came to our HQ. So we *are* on the right track. But it's getting late. We'll pick up on it again tomorrow morning. Uh . . . except there's one more thing for *you* to do, Officer Rockaway."

"Oh?"

"Yes. As word expert. I want you to go straight to the library and get that book—*Tales of Mystery*, was it?"

"*And Imagination*, yeah," I said cautiously. "By Edgar Allan Poe."

"Right. And then read those tales Mr. Smith mentions and give us a rundown on them tomorrow. A *detailed* rundown. I have a hunch there might be something in them he was pointing to. Maybe the best clue yet."

I left for the library with mixed feelings. I mean, here we were in the middle of summer vacation, and the jerk was giving me a book-report assignment!

But half an hour later I had a complete change of heart. I'd hardly gotten out of the library, flipping over the pages and thinking what a lot of reading I had ahead of me, when I saw—there, standing out and almost screaming at me, in block capitals plus quotation marks—well, *this:*

"WILLIAM LEGRAND."

I mean, it hadn't just been written in pencil or ink by some present-day borrower. It was printed. Part of the story. Part of a story written almost exactly a century and a half ago by Edgar Allan Poe himself.

It was like a voice from the grave!

As if the guy whose cabin we'd just been searching had all the time been bricked up inside that *tale!*

· 8 ·

The Gold-Bug

It must have shown on my face when I arrived at our HQ next morning.

"You found something, Officer Rockaway?" said McGurk.

"Did I *find* something!" I said, hurrying to my seat. "I now know what *G-B* stands for!"

"You do?" said McGurk.

"I thought you were supposed to be reporting on those stories," said Brains.

"I *am*," I said. "That's where I found out about *G-B*. And you can settle your mind once and for all—it isn't Gerald Bellingham."

"Go *on*, Officer Rockaway!" said McGurk, thumping the table.

"One minute," I said. "Do you have **Mr.** Byrne's copy of the shopping list handy?"

"Right here," McGurk said, reaching to the box labeled CURRENT CASE—EVIDENCE & CLUES, and fishing out the Sheldon Byrne Agency memo slip.

"Okay," I said. "Well, of course, the original shopping list is still at the cabin. But here's a copy of those initials as they appear on *that* list. The way Bill Smith wrote them."

And I pushed forward a page from my notebook:

"And on this other page"—I pushed that forward, too—"here's my copy of the way they appeared on Mr. Byrne's list."

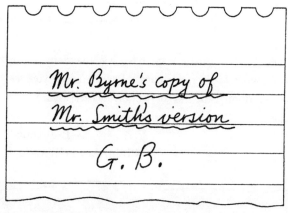

Mr. Byrne's copy of
Mr. Smith's version

G. B.

They stared at the two sets of initials.

"Well?" said McGurk.

"Well," I said. "Mr. Byrne copied them wrong. That shouldn't be a *period* between the *G* and the *B*. The way Bill Smith himself had it, it was a *hyphen*."

A murmur arose. But it was still a mystified murmur.

"And you know what it stood for?" I said. "*Gold-Bug!* To be exact, 'The Gold-Bug.' The title of one of those *Tales of Mystery and Imagination!*"

Never had any bunch of kids listened so intently to a book report. Because as soon as I'd delivered that first whammy, I followed up with another.

"Just look at *this*!"

And I opened the book, which I'd marked at the place, and let my discovery leap out at *them*.

It was at the end of a letter written by one of the characters. And here's a copy:

"If you can, in any way, make it convenient, come over with Jupiter. *Do* come. I wish to see you *to-night,* upon business of importance. I assure you that it is of the *highest* importance.

—Ever yours,
"WILLIAM LEGRAND."

There was an awed silence. I broke it myself.

"I guess this was where Bill Smith got his pen name."

"It sure seems like it. . . ." McGurk looked dazed.

"And guess where the story's supposed to take place?" I said. (I mean—oh boy!—this was the word expert's big moment, all right!)

"Where?" whispered McGurk, almost *humbly.*

"South Carolina. Near Charleston. Where Mr. Byrne said Bill Smith started as a cub reporter."

Wanda cleared her throat. "I guess he was hooked on Edgar Allan Poe even then."

"Very likely." But I still wasn't through. "And guess what kind of a guy this William Legrand in the story was?"

"What kind?" said Mari.

"A recluse! Living in a hut in some woods!"

I leaned back, enjoying my triumph.

"So what is this story, this—this 'Gold-Bug,' *about*?" asked McGurk.

"Buried treasure," I said. "Pirates' loot, buried for years. This character finds a scrap of parchment with a message in code, and he cracks that code. And it says in the preface that this code, which Poe invented, was so good it became the basis for the Morse code itself and—"

"Officer Rockaway!"

I stopped. "Sorry, McGurk!" I mumbled. "You have a question?"

"Darned right I do!" he said. "Where and how did he find the treasure?"

"Under a tulip tree. A *special* tulip tree with a human skull nailed to one of its limbs. The seventh limb on its eastern fork, and—"

"Officer Grieg," McGurk cut in, "did you notice a tulip tree yesterday?"

"No," she said. "But I wouldn't be surprised if there was one *somewhere* in the woods."

"Right!" McGurk shot to his feet. "That's it, men! Nice work, Officer Rockaway! Let's get rolling. Get your bikes and—" He frowned. "Did anyone notice any spades up at the cabin? There's bound to be, I suppose, but—oh, forget it! We'll bring our own. Spades, trowels, anything to dig with."

59

"But don't you want to hear the rest of my report?"

"Not now, Officer Rockaway! This has just got to be the breakthrough we're looking for. Come on, men!"

Well, I didn't care for *that*. I mean, who'd been up in his room all evening poring over the small print of an old beat-up copy of Poe's *Tales* while they'd been watching TV or playing computer games?

I did manage to mention one more fact I'd discovered, though.

"We'd better take something for cutting the undergrowth."

"What undergrowth?" McGurk said, stopping in his tracks.

"Over the spot where the treasure—uh—stash is buried. In the story, the Legrand character took a scythe."

McGurk's lip curled. "Officer Rockaway, you're thinking like a book reporter, not a working detective. He needed the scythe because the treasure had been buried there for years, right?"

"Right," this working detective mumbled.

"Well, *our* Bill Legrand has buried *his* stash more recently. And he'll have had to clear the ground himself before digging the hole. So it should be all the easier to spot, once we've found the tulip tree."

"Yes," said Wanda. "And that reminds me, McGurk.

Just give me ten minutes to run home and change my shoes and put on some old—"

"*Change,* Officer Grieg?"

"Yes, McGurk," said Wanda firmly. "Climbing a tulip tree isn't the same as climbing any old tree. You need to be properly equipped."

"Well, okay. You're the expert. Ten minutes and no longer."

Wanda was back well within the time limit, dressed in her oldest, raggediest jeans and wearing her thickest-soled sneakers. Then we were on our way, cheeks flushed and eyes gleaming, some with spades strapped to our bikes, others with trowels, just like a bunch of prospectors ourselves—bitten by the gold-bug.

· 9 ·

The Tulip Tree

As soon as we reached the cabin and parked our bikes, we plunged into the woods along the nearest path. Almost immediately it began to rise between beech trees.

There were lots of tripping roots, but the ground was pretty bare of undergrowth. Also, it was soft with layers of rotted leaves, and I couldn't help hoping the tulip tree would be nearby, where digging would be easy.

But no. That path soon dipped and twisted down again. Here, in places, it became almost lost in under-growth that was still drenched, and our feet and legs began to get cold and wet. Fortunately, no really tall trees grew here, let alone a tulip tree, so we didn't have to hang around getting wetter and colder. Which is why some of us weren't too pleased when McGurk suddenly stopped and put a finger to his lips.

A swishing sound was coming from behind a nearby thicket.

"Somebody spying on us?" whispered Brains. "Somebody—?"

Before McGurk could hush him up, the steps became hurried, and soon faded out of earshot.

"Probably a deer," said Wanda.

"Yeah," grunted McGurk, shrugging. "Come on, men. I think I see a clearing ahead."

We hurried along, only too anxious to get out of that undergrowth. The trees thinned. We began to step on some kind of short, springy, creeping plants. But the grass toward the center of the clearing was long and lush—and very wet.

Except at the center itself. Here it was stamped down and there was what looked like the remains of a campfire—a black circle of charred wood and ashes, with crushed empty beer cans scattered around it.

"Looks like a teenagers' hangout," murmured McGurk, leaning on his spade.

"That is what I think, too," said Mari. "It sounds close to a road just here."

Traffic noises were drifting through the trees.

Suddenly Wanda groaned. "I'm stupid! I've just re-membered—tulip trees *prefer* clearings like this, where they get plenty of sun." She glanced around. "There isn't one here. But *that's* what we should be aiming for. Clearings."

"*Now* she tells us!" grumbled Brains, looking down at a tear in his jeans where they'd been caught on a thorn.

"Better yet," McGurk said to Wanda, "why don't we start patrolling the *edge* of the woods? There's always plenty of sun there. I mean, finding clearings inside woods without a map—well, you could get soaked."

"Not to mention poisoned with ivy," I said.

Anyway, McGurk's suggestion put us all in a more hopeful mood. Brains even stopped fussing and remem-bered he'd brought along his pocket compass.

"It'll point us to the south boundary," he said, study-ing the flickering needle. "Around from the southeast to the northwest, that's where the sun strikes most."

"Just what *I* was thinking," said McGurk.

Well, we had to beat our way through a few more patches of wet undergrowth, but it wasn't long before we reached a point where the woods gave ground to fields and the sun was blazing down.

"This is more like it, Officer Grieg!" said McGurk.

We murmured our agreement as the steam began to rise from our legs.

"Yes, McGurk!" Wanda said. "And it looks like we got lucky right away!" She was pointing to a tree about two hundred yards ahead.

There was no missing it. It soared above all the others, standing like a sentinel where the woods parted to allow the entrance of a much broader path. There was a horse barn in the nearby field, with this wider, churned-up track leading directly into the woods.

But our attention was mostly fixed high up. As we approached that dense canopy of leaves, birds arose from inside it, protesting. Mainly crows, possibly grackles—black anyway—along with a few jays. Personally, I half expected to see a raven among them, but guessed that this was because the case was beginning to get to me.

"I guess this case is—," I began.

"Be quiet, please!" said Wanda. "I have a problem here!" She was gazing at the trunk.

Right enough, it went up a long way without presenting her with any side limbs or stumps. Making up for that, though—well, Willie said it for us: "Somebody's made some steps!"

Wanda flicked back her hair. "They aren't steps. They're what's left of some old birdhouses."

We saw what she meant: Rusted iron brackets with

chunks of broken wood still clinging to them, every few feet up the trunk.

"I'm just wondering how safe they'll be," she murmured.

"Huh . . . well . . . proceed with caution then, Officer Grieg."

"Don't worry, McGurk," Wanda replied, reaching up to the first of these "steps."

When she'd given it a good tugging, she seemed satisfied.

"Here we go!" she sang out, hauling herself upward and heading for the second, digging her heels into the rough bark to get maximum leverage on the way.

We watched as she proceeded from "step" to "step" slowly—taking no chances—but steadily, until she'd reached the first limbs, twenty to thirty feet above our heads.

"You okay, Officer Grieg?"

"I am *now*," she called down, swinging into the foliage.

"Well, don't forget," I yelled back. "Take the east fork—that's the one on your left—and it's—"

"I know, I know!" her voice came down. "It's the seventh limb on that fork."

"But check out the sixth and eighth also!" yelled

McGurk. "He might have nailed the skull to one of *them* by mistake."

Myself, I couldn't see Bill Smith nailing a skull to *anything* that high up. My memory of him was still vague, but an agile, muscular athlete he definitely was *not*. He—

That was when we heard the thudding of hooves and turned and saw a horse approaching along the track out of the woods, kicking up withered scraps of fallen tuliptree flowers.

"What are you doing?" said the rider, in a harsh, challenging voice.

It took me a second or two to recognize her. Then I realized it was Ruth Pawling, one of the snootiest seniors at the high school. And I must say she looked pretty fearsome, with her shiny leather riding boots, her black jockey cap, and a nasty-looking riding crop.

"I said, what do you think you're doing?" she repeated, with a twitch of that crop.

Yeah! the glossy dark-brown horse seemed to say, giving the ground a stomp.

Willie backed away in alarm. "We're looking for a skull!" he blurted. "It—"

"Officer Sandowsky!" hissed McGurk. Then he looked up at the frowning girl.

"We're seeing if we can find out where Mr. Smith went," he said. "The—the guy who lived in the cabin."

"Well, he won't be up *there!*" she said. "Besides, he's been gone for weeks. And I don't believe you! You're trespassing, and I'm going to tell my grandfather. He'll—"

"That's quite all right, my dear!"

We spun around.

It was Mr. Logan, in his jogging gear again, coming out of the woods.

"They're here with Mr. Byrne's permission." He turned to us. "Any luck?" His eyes flickered across the spades and trowels we'd laid on the ground.

As if in answer, Wanda's voice came floating down. "There's no skull up here, McGurk! . . . Oh! Hello!" she said, emerging from the foliage and reaching for the top bracket with her foot.

"Skull?" said Mr. Logan, giving McGurk a sharp look.

"Just a hunch, sir," said McGurk, coloring. "Like—like—"

"Well—like *what?*"

McGurk took a deep breath. "Like maybe Mr. Smith climbed up there. Maybe to look around. And maybe he had a heart attack. And just managed to strap himself to a limb. By—by his belt. Then died. Out of sight of anyone down here—and—and—"

"Yeah!" said Willie. "And his flesh began to rot away, and the crows came and stripped his skull bare, and—"

"Willie! *Please!*" Wanda called down. "I can hear every word, and it spoils my concentration!"

Mr. Logan looked thoughtful, glancing from Willie to McGurk. "Hmm! It's one possibility, of course."

Wanda was coming down the trunk as slowly as she'd climbed it. Step by extremely cautious step.

"So *that's* how you got up there," said Mr. Logan.

"Yes, sir," said Wanda. "But . . . they were broken . . . already."

"I know, I know," said the old jogger sadly. "It's years since they were in regular use. . . . I put them up myself. . . . Tenth birthday present for Ruthie here. . . . Different levels, different birds." He, too, was speaking in jerks, watching Wanda's every move. "You're stepping on the old crested-flycatcher shelf right now. . . . And . . . there you go! That's what's left of the bluebirds' house."

Wanda lightly jumped down from there. "Really, sir? You made them all?"

"Sure did!"

"Well, it's a good thing for me you went as high as you did!" she said, pointing to the top "step."

"Yes, but not for the other birds, I'm afraid," said Mr. Logan. "An American kestrel took that one over. And he used the nest boxes below as corporate lunchrooms. Bluebird on the menu today, down on the second floor . . . tomorrow's special: tender baby flickers on the fifth. Heh-heh!"

To me, there was something chilling about this powerful old lawyer who seemed to admire a bird of prey's swooping down on his small neighbors and eating them.

"But *skulls*?" he murmured, shaking his head. "The corpses of missing persons?"

"Dumb kids!" said Ruth. "I'm going. Come on, Chaser!" And she jerked the horse's head in a homeward direction.

"Wait for me, my dear!" said the old man.

As we watched them enter the barn, McGurk said, "I took a quick look around while all the yacking was going on. I couldn't see any place where Mr. Smith might have dug a hole this side of the tree. But let's take a look at the other side."

·10·

Another Digger?

But that was no good, either. After about twenty minutes of careful searching, McGurk had to admit defeat.

"It looks like we've brought our spades and trowels for nothing!"

"Ah, yes! That reminds me, Chief McGurk," said Mari. "Mr. Logan. Did you see the way he looked at our spades? I expected him to ask us about them, he seemed so curious."

While McGurk's freckles were still bunching up in a deep frown, Mari went on, "He told us yesterday he is usually very quick to pounce on anything like that."

71

McGurk nodded slowly. "Yeah . . . but if you remember, Officer Yoshimura, just when he noticed the digging tools, Officer Grieg came down blabbering about a skull. That was enough to drive spades out of anyone's mind."

I agreed. "You're right. Especially when Willie started getting all gruesome about birds stripping the flesh off corpses' heads!"

"But that's what you said happened in the story!" Willie protested. "When I asked you on the way here. You—"

"Don't tell me *you kids* are digging for truffles, too?"

We turned. It was Ruth Pawling. This time she was on foot and alone. No one had heard her approach.

"Sorry?" said McGurk.

"Truffle hunting!" she said, tapping the riding crop against one of her boots. "Digging for them. Is that *your* story, too? As well as looking for Mr. Smith?"

"Truffles?" said Willie. "You mean some kinda chocolate candy?"

"Foolish child!" she said. "Truffles are a very special kind of fungus. A very expensive delicacy. We sometimes have them at the country club's restaurant."

"Oh, yes, of course!" said Wanda, with a flick of her hair. "*I've* heard of them. They grow in forests. People use special dogs to sniff them out."

"Is that a fact?" said Willie, wide-eyed.

"But mainly in Europe," said Wanda. "I didn't think they grew over *here.*"

"Me either," said Ruth Pawling, coldly eyeing our spades and trowels.

"Just a sec!" said McGurk. "You talk like someone else has been digging around here."

"Yes," said Ruth. "A woman. Further into the trees. The day before yesterday. Grungy old jeans. Black sweater full of holes and food stains. And dirty sneakers. One of these nature freaks." She glanced at Wanda. "Like *her.*"

"Who are *you* calling—?"

"Quiet, Officer Grieg!" McGurk turned to Ruth. "Digging, you say?"

"Well, armed with a trowel and a plastic bag. We don't mind people coming and picking berries and things. But Grandfather draws the line at people rooting up plants."

"So how did you know she was looking for truffles?" said McGurk.

"She told me. When I challenged her. She was quite

rude about it, too." Ruth's eyes flashed, and she gave her boot another whack.

"What did she look like?" said McGurk. "I mean *exactly.*"

"Oh, just some scruffy hippie type. Very short haircut. I don't mean *fashionable* short. More like she'd had it done in a marine boot camp." Ruth sniffed. "We get that kind around occasionally. Grandfather even thought one had broken into the cabin yesterday. Anyway, what *are* you digging for?"

"Indian remains."

I gasped. McGurk's split-second promptness had taken my breath away.

"*What* Indian remains?" said Ruth.

"Mohawk," he said—again without a moment's hesitation. "They used to hunt in these parts, didn't they?"

"Huh! You sound as wacky as that woman!" Ruth turned in disgust and stalked back toward the horse barn.

"McGurk!" said Wanda. "I'd never have believed you could look someone in the eye and tell such a whopper as *that!*"

"Me either, Chief McGurk!" said Mari reproachfully. "And it *sounded* so truthful!"

"Well, so it was, Officer Yoshimura!" He appealed to

us all. "Don't you remember Lieutenant Carmichael? In the TV series? His mother was a full-blooded Mohawk. And—and I bet you anything there'll be at least one Lieutenant Carmichael book among those manuscripts!"

Well, there was no arguing against that. But it wasn't helping us in our search.

And neither was the weather. Just then, the edge of a huge black cloud came looming up, sending us scurrying on our way, hoping the rain would hold off until we found some really solid shelter.

The horse barn itself was out of the question, of course. But luckily it wasn't far from there to the other end of the dirt road that ran through the woods. We reached the cabin with only seconds to spare before that old black cloud burst.

Now let's get this straight.

Most gold prospectors used to be equipped with maps of some kind, however crude. We'd rushed into *our* search mapless.

As a result, we'd wandered off in a totally wrong direction that morning. We couldn't really be blamed for this. As far as we knew, there *was* no map of those woods. But I'm pleased to announce that there is one now. Thanks to that first blundering exploration, I was able to draw it up later, and here it is:

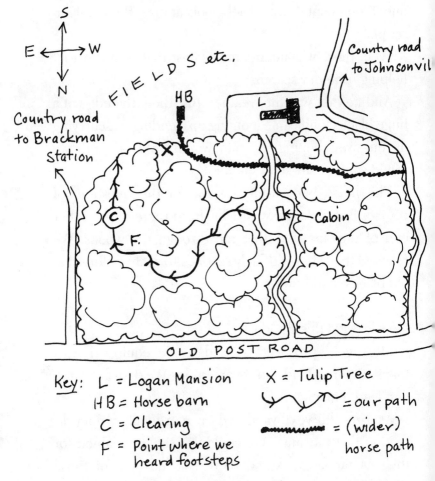

Key: L = Logan Mansion   X = Tulip Tree
HB = Horse barn   = our path
C = Clearing
F = Point where we   = (wider)
heard footsteps   horse path

MAP OF LOGAN WOODS by JR

It doesn't show all the paths—just those we followed and the wider one we came across near the tulip tree. If only we'd known about that horse path at the start, you can imagine the time and trouble it would have saved us. We didn't even realize what a useful shortcut back to the cabin it would make, with that huge, threatening cloud hanging over us.

Anyway, we reached the cabin just in time, so that was all right, and for the first few minutes we simply sat around getting our breaths back and thinking about our mistakes. Also thanking our lucky stars that we hadn't gotten even wetter, as we listened to the rain drumming on the roof.

Some of us sat on the edge of the table, swinging our still-damp legs. Wanda had chosen the painted chair, straddling it and leaning forward with her arms folded across its back, letting her hair hang down. Mari had found a stool in the corner next to the bookshelf and the telephone.

As for the big overstuffed armchair—well, there's no need to tell you who'd grabbed *that*!

He was the first to speak. "As soon as this shower's over, we'd better go see if there's another tulip tree, men. Sounds like we might have some competition."

"Who?" said Brains.

"The truffle woman, of course!" said McGurk.

"I was just thinking Ruth probably made that up," I said. "As an excuse to ask about *our* digging plans. Probably her grandfather sent her across."

"No, Joey," said Mari. "I think *she* was telling the truth."

"Yeah," said McGurk. "It sounds like the race is now on to find the right tulip tree."

He glanced at the window, but the rain was showing no sign of letting up.

"Well, I've been thinking, too," said Wanda. "Just because Edgar Allan Poe had a skull nailed to the tulip tree, it doesn't mean that Mr. Smith nailed one to *his* tree."

"Oh?" said McGurk.

"No," replied Wanda. "All he wanted to do was draw our attention to a tulip tree, right? Well, there can't be *that* many here, in these parts."

"There's one in Willow Park," I said.

"Oh, sure!" she said. "And I can see him burying his stash in a public place!"

"The guy in the Felon's Fiddle case did," I retorted.

"Yes," said Wanda. "But *his* was only in a tiny bottle. This is a large suitcase. It would take him hours."

"Hey, maybe not!" said Brains. "How about if he transferred his manuscripts to microfilm? That would fit inside a small bottle as easily as the Felon's Fiddle diamonds."

Willie sighed. "I liked it best with the skull nailed to the limb."

"Whatever," said McGurk. "But right now, while it's pouring down, we might as well be thinking about some of those other stories on the tape."

"About time, too!"

"Okay, Officer Rockaway. So go ahead with your book report."

"Well," I began, " 'The Black Cat' you already know about."

Mari, who'd been trying the phone and shaking her head, made the wall behind me say, "Meeeow!"

"Cut it out, Officer Yoshimura!" snapped McGurk. He stared at her. "Anyway, what's with the phone?"

"It is dead, Chief McGurk."

McGurk shrugged. "Probably Mr. Smith has it cut off at the exchange when he goes on a trip. So no burglars can call to check whether he's home or not." He turned to me. "Go on with your report, Officer Rockaway. What about 'The Stolen Letter'?"

"'The *Purloined* Letter,'" I said. "Yes. Well. They knew the guy who'd swiped it. They knew it was somewhere in his office. So they had it searched from top to bottom. By experts. Result: zilch!"

"*And?*" said McGurk, looking extremely interested.

"So Edgar Allan Poe's great detective, Auguste Dupin, is called in."

"And did *he* find it?" said McGurk.

"You bet!"

"Where?" said Wanda.

"In the most obvious place of all. On a letter rack hanging from the mantelpiece." Five pairs of eyes swiveled to the fireplace. "The kind of rack people used for everyday bits of paper like bills, business cards, raffle tickets. And this letter, which was of the very highest importance—"

"Yes? Go on!"

"The crook had stuffed it into a cheap torn envelope, making it look like a piece of junk mail."

"Great!" said Wanda. "So all *we* need to do is look for a twenty-pound suitcase hanging from his bulletin board!"

"Not so fast, Officer Grieg!" McGurk turned back to me. "You say the room was searched by experts?"

"Yeah," I said. "Poe describes all the cunning hiding places that really smart crooks might use indoors. And all the cunning methods that really smart cops might use to track them down without tearing the place apart."

"Like what?"

"Like taking very accurate measurements of drawers and then of the desks they fit into. To see if there's space been left for secret compartments. Or to test if chair legs have been hollowed out—"

"To conceal suitcases!" jeered Wanda. "Yeah!"

"Or *microfilm,* don't forget," said Brains.

McGurk looked very thoughtful as he glanced around the room. "Well, maybe . . . ," he murmured. "But don't forget what Mr. Byrne said about fire risk. I still think the stash will be found someplace *outside.* Good work, though, Officer Rockaway. Sounds like searching a room with precision instruments might make a useful training session someday." This produced groans. "Anyway, forget about the stash itself, men. Just keep looking for any more clues he might have left behind. That's what we're most likely to find in here."

"Yes. We haven't finished with the shopping list yet," I said.

And I'd only just stepped into the kitchen to take a closer look when Mari's yell had me hurrying back.

She doesn't usually yell, even when she gets excited. But she did this time.

"Heyeee!" she yelled, drawing it out in a way that made it sound all the more urgent. "Look at *this,* Chief McGurk!"

She was holding the phone in one hand and the cord in the other.

And they weren't connected!

81

"This wasn't switched off at the exchange!" she said. "This cord has been pulled out by the—the roots!" The bare wires were sticking out at the end of the cord. "Whoever did it must have pushed it back in the hole without troubling to connect it up properly, Chief McGurk!"

"Yeah," growled McGurk. "So no one would notice until it was too late." His face was grim. "Which backs my hunch that Bill Smith *was* kidnapped, men! That they burst in and ripped the cord out before he had time to dial nine-one-one!"

·11·

The Membership Card

"C-can you fix it, Brains?" Willie whispered. "In case we need to call emergency?"

"Well," said Brains, "I'll need my special tools to—"

"Leave it for now, Officer Bellingham!" said McGurk. "Let's stay with this new line of inquiry, men. Keep your eyes peeled for any *other* signs of a struggle. Maybe splashes of blood. Even stray bullet holes. And you keep your *nose* peeled, Officer Sandowsky. Cleaning fluid used to remove bloodstains . . ."

So that close room-searching session took place earlier than we'd expected—and for real: checking out chairs, crawling on floorboards, sniffing at rugs, craning to the ceilings. McGurk himself went over that armchair inch by inch. Then he concentrated on all the cushions and pillows in the cabin, muttering, "They mighta used something like this as a silencer."

But without results.

In fact, it was toward the end—when I was beginning to put the violent-kidnap theory down to McGurk's lurid imagination—that I turned back to the shopping list.

Magazines in particular.

Why had Bill Smith written just *that* down—*Magazines?*

What was he referring to?

So far, we hadn't come across any pile of regular-type magazines—*TV Guide, House and Garden, Playboy,* newspaper color supplements. There weren't any even under the cushion of the armchair.

But then I remembered something.

I turned to the shelf of old paperbacks. And there, sure enough, I found them! A bunch of three or four *Mystery Magazines,* which come out monthly but look just like regular paperback novels.

"Come on, Officer Rockaway!" growled McGurk. "This isn't the time to catch up on your reading!"

I sighed and was just about to put the magazines back

when my eye was caught by the title of a story on the cover of one of them. This:

"Felicity Snell's First Case," by BILL LEGRAND
A little-known story by the master...............page 35.

Well, I didn't have to look for the page. The magazine fell open at the right place. And *that* was because of a small, grubby, dog-eared card that must have been used as a bookmark.

"Look at *this*, McGurk! Two items on his shopping list in one!"

"Huh?"

"*Magazines* and *Renew membership!*"

And here's a photocopy. First, the front:

And, more important, the back, where this penciled note had been scribbled:

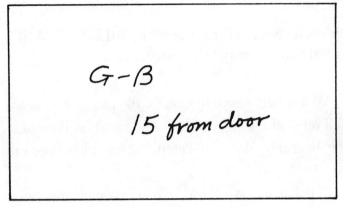

"Well, at least we know what he *looks* like now," said Willie.

"That isn't his *ID* picture!" I said. "That's the Mystery Writers of America logo. That's Edgar Allan Poe."

"Forget that!" said McGurk. "What about these things he's written on the back?"

"*G-B* again," murmured Brains.

"With a hyphen," I reminded him.

" 'The Gold-Bug,' " said Wanda. "Why would he draw our attention to it *again*?"

"It just shows how important to him that clue must have been," said McGurk. "But . . . what does a *door* have to do with it? Tulip trees don't have doors."

"What if he meant the door to one of the bird-houses?" said Willie.

"Uh-uh," said Wanda. "Those birdhouses didn't have any doors left. Most are just entrance holes, anyway."

"You're right," said McGurk. "I think he meant an ordinary door."

"Why put *G-B* again, then?" Brains insisted.

"I've already told you," said McGurk. "Because it's such an important clue. To remind us that it's a buried treasure stash we're looking for. But"—he frowned—"I wonder what door he *meant*? The cabin door? That seems the most likely. . . ."

"Yes," said Wanda. "But which one? The front? The back? The cellar?"

"And fifteen *what*?" said Brains. "Inches? Feet? Yards?"

"It won't be *inches*," said McGurk. "Fifteen inches from a door might be okay for a very small object. A diamond ring or something. But not for a suitcase. It's got to be feet or yards."

"Or meters," said Brains.

"Okay, them, too, maybe. Anyway"—McGurk glanced at the window—"the rain's stopped and it's time for lunch. So what you do, Officer Bellingham—since you're our science expert and know so much about measuring—you bring back with you a string fifteen yards long. Precisely. Got it?"

Brains nodded. "But—"

"And you put knots in it. Every three feet. Then we can use it to measure with either way. Fifteen yards or fifteen feet."

"What about meters?" said Brains.

"Make the whole thing fifteen *meters* long then!" said McGurk. "Then we'll have fifteen yards, fifteen feet, and fifteen meters all marked out, ready."

"And bring some stakes or pegs," I said. "To fix it in the ground."

"All right, all right!" said Brains. "I know *my* job! You just stick to yours!"

"If it hadn't been for *me*," I began, "we'd never—"

"Cut it out!" said McGurk. "We *all* have our jobs to do. And, by golly, now that we've got the best lead so far, we all pull *together*! So let's go. I want you all back here by one-thirty sharp!"

·12·

Brains Pulls Out All the Stops

At the end of the last chapter I gave the impression that I didn't think much of Brains as a science expert. Well, now I have to correct that and hand it to him for the professional way he prepared to tackle this particular job. I mean, he didn't turn up after lunch with *any* old piece of string. Oh, no! He came equipped with a length of green gardening twine, neatly wound around a piece of wood. At the loose end he'd made a firm loop, large enough to slip over a doorknob.

Then he'd marked off the required lengths. But not

with knots. Knots wouldn't have been very easy to see. So our science expert used brightly colored paint. With a blob of yellow at precisely fifteen feet, orange at the fifteen-yard point, and red to mark the fifteen-meter spot.

When he'd shown us this, I pointed to the black plastic bag from which he'd taken it and said (very humbly), "And I suppose the stakes or pegs are in there, Brains?"

"Stakes or pegs!" he jeered. "What *for*, stakes or pegs?"

"To mark out the points on the ground that are fifteen feet—or yards, or meters—from the door."

"Amateurs!" Brains plunged a hand into the sack. "*This* is what I've brought for that job."

"Birdseed?" said Wanda, staring at the heap in the palm of his hand.

"From the big sack in our garage," said Brains. "Dad buys it from the Audubon Center for our bird feeders."

"So?" growled McGurk.

"Well, at first I thought of using a bag of confetti that Mom still had left over from my cousin Kelly's wedding. But that wouldn't have been environmentally friendly."

"Environmentally friendly?" said Wanda. "What *are* you talking about?"

"Sprinkling confetti on the ground. *You'd* have been the first to complain, Wanda Grieg! But"—Brains sprinkled some of the seeds in a thin line—"using these, we can mark out our fifteen-foot circles—or semicircles—and the birds and chipmunks will clear up afterward."

"Officer Bellingham, you've done real good!" said McGurk. "Now let's get to work!"

As Brains fixed the loop to the front doorknob, Mari said, "It must have taken you most of your lunch break to get all this ready, Gerald."

"You can say *that* again!" he grunted, pulling the loop tight and beginning to unwind the string. "One lousy peanut-butter sandwich is all I had time for. But"—he placed the string on the ground at the fifteen-foot mark and sprinkled some of the seed there—"first things first."

"And at least the *birds* won't go hungry," murmured Wanda as Brains moved on, keeping the string tight and depositing his thin trail of seeds.

As I said, it was a very professional piece of work. Here's a map I made later, showing the way it functioned:

PLAN OF CLEARING by $\mathcal{R}$

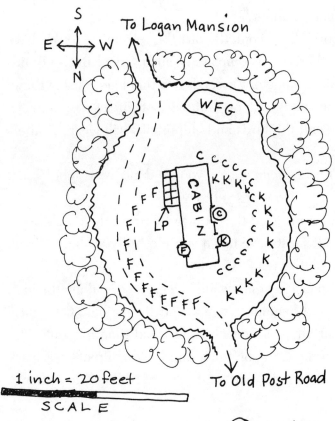

To Logan Mansion

To Old Post Road

1 inch = 20 feet

SCALE

Key:

〰〰〰 = Edge of woods

WFG = Wildflower Garden

▦ LP = Log pile

Ⓕ = Front door

F F F F F = 15 ft. line from front door

Ⓚ = Kitchen door

K K K K k = 15 ft. line from kitchen door

Ⓒ = Cellar door

c c c c = 15 ft. line from cellar door

┊ ┊ = continuation of dirt road inside Clearing

As you can see, all the fifteen-foot points fell inside the clearing, making them easy to chart. Unfortunately, it didn't make our *search* much easier, because they all fell on ground that was hard and obviously undisturbed by any recent digging.

Like those that were fifteen feet from the front door—most of them in the continuation of the dirt road, which was much too hard for digging, what with the passage of vehicles over it. And in back, where the ground sloped up to the trees, there was a lot of granite outcrop, especially toward the edge of the woods. Which was precisely where most of the points fell that came fifteen feet from either the kitchen or cellar doors.

No. There was really only one likely spot inside that clearing. And after we'd prodded and probed at the hard ground on both sides, McGurk suddenly yelled, "Of *course*! *This* is where it'll be, men!"

A chipmunk gave a squeak of alarm and dove for cover as McGurk strode toward the woodpile and tore off the tarpaulin cover.

"Come on!" he said, beginning to toss the logs to one side. "Don't just stand there. Help me clear these away. The stash has just got to be under here."

It didn't take us long to dismantle that pile. But, alas, the only things that had *just got* to be under there were two more chipmunks and several spiders—and they were very soon *out* of there. Besides them, there was just a mess of dead leaves and rotted wood, and, below that—

"Concrete!" Wanda groaned.

She was right. Either Bill Smith or some previous tenant had tried to cut down the wood-rotting risk by laying down a protective foundation.

And this wasn't recently laid concrete, either. *This* had been down there for years. Chipped and cracked in places, sure—but only slightly. Not as a result of someone whacking it with a sledgehammer to make way for excavating a hole.

"Oh, all right, men!" grumbled McGurk, looking bitterly disappointed. "Get 'em back in a pile!"

After that, we turned our attention to the fifteen-*yard* points, and that was even more frustrating. Because from whichever door we measured *them,* they all fell way beyond the clearing and into the woods. Which not only had us tangling with undergrowth and thorns and stuff again, but we also had the tree trunks themselves to contend with.

I mean, we couldn't just stretch the string out to the required length and freely trace out a circle with it *there.* We had to keep going in and out—one fifteen-yard spot at a time.

"Argh! Forget it!" groaned McGurk, after we'd been

94

working on this for most of the rest of the afternoon. "It *has* to be feet."

"But we've already *tried* feet," said Brains. "So—"

"If you dare to say *meters*, Officer Bellingham, I'll bust you! They're even longer than yards!"

"All I was going to say was this," muttered Brains. "He must have meant some other *door.* A door where there *is* a clear space in front of it. Where you can measure fifteen feet *and* fifteen yards without trees and concrete and stuff getting in the way." His eyes rolled defiantly. "Yes. And fifteen *meters*, too!"

"But this door has to be close enough for him to keep tabs on his stash, Officer Bellingham!"

"Is the horse barn close enough?" said Brains.

There was a short silence, broken only by the squabbling of some purple finches and sparrows as they began their seed-clearing operation.

Then McGurk gave a shout of joy. "Officer Bellingham, I think you've hit on it! *Great* thinking! . . . Now let's hope Ruth Pawling's gone out riding!"

Well, I guess luck just wasn't on our side that afternoon.

Ruth *had* gone out horseback riding, yes. But only as far as the field itself. We watched from the woods as she put Chaser through his paces, going around and around and jumping some brushwood hurdles.

It was painful to watch. I mean, there we were, itching to get on with our search—fifteen feet, fifteen yards, and fifteen meters from that barn door, over lovely level turf, so easy to dig holes in.

But it wasn't to be.

"Huh!" grunted Wanda. "She looks set for hours!"

"Yeah," said Brains. "And I'm getting hungry!"

McGurk sighed. "Okay, men. We might as well call it a day. But first thing tomorrow, we'll give it another spin. We're so close to that stash now, I can almost smell it."

"*I* can't," said Willie. "But I do keep catching a whiff of broiled steak." He nodded toward the woods behind us. "I think someone must be having a cookout, and it's driving me crazy!"

None of the rest of us could smell it, but his words were enough to set Brains's stomach rumbling alarmingly.

"Yes," I said, starting to salivate, "let's go home."

·13·

A Surprise Visitor

I'm beginning to think this isn't such a good idea after all!" Wanda said the next morning. We were in the horse-barn field and we'd completed the fifteen-yard semicircle. It had proved just as unsuccessful as our investigation into the fifteen-foot one half an hour earlier. And the fifteen-meter semicircle looked like it would be yet another turkey.

"I mean, there's no sign of any of the grass being disturbed, except by horses' hooves," she went on. "And besides"—she looked around at the empty barn, at the edge of the trees, and at the Logan mansion behind its white picket fence—"it's too exposed here. Ruth and Chaser could come cantering out of the woods any minute. Mr. Logan could leap over the fence. Any of the help could look across from the upper windows. And here we'd be. Caught."

McGurk frowned. "Well . . . that's a risk we've just got to take, Officer Grieg."

"I know," said Wanda. "But *Mr. Smith* didn't have to. *He* could have been spotted anytime, too, when he was burying his stash. I don't think he meant this door at all."

"Well, maybe you're right. But—"

Which was when we *were* spotted.

"Hey!" shouted Ruth, emerging from the trees and spurring Chaser into a gallop. "What are you doing *here*?"

"Uh-oh!" said Brains.

"And what's *he* doing with that string?" Ruth added, reaching our group and pulling on Chaser's reins so that he reared up menacingly.

"Continuing our investigation," said McGurk, not looking any too happy about the horse's flared nostrils and bared teeth.

"Huh!" grunted Ruth. "Indian remains, I suppose?"

"Yes," said McGurk.

Then Ruth had us all gaping up at her. "I see," she murmured. "Yesterday I thought you were just getting smart with me. But my grandfather says you might be on to something. He says he did hear rumors as a boy that a Mohawk chief was buried in these woods."

As I say, we gaped at her.

She smiled—thinly, sourly; almost against her will, it seemed.

"So he says I've got to let you get on with it. And to tell you, with his compliments, that he naturally expects you to inform him if you should find something. *If*," she added haughtily, no doubt on her own behalf.

On our way back from the barn, shortly afterward, Wanda made a suggestion.

"Hey! Hold it a minute!" We'd just reached the clearing. "What about *paces*?"

"Same as yards," grunted Brains.

"Not with *your* little legs," said Wanda. "Or Mari's."

"What are you getting at, Officer Grieg?" said McGurk.

"I mean, Mr. Smith may have had these two in mind. He *had* seen us, don't forget. *G-B* might stand for Gerald Bellingham, after all."

"But—" I began.

"I mean *as well as* 'Gold-Bug,'" said Wanda.

"Do you have anything special in mind, Officer Grieg?"

"Yes." Wanda pointed to the wildflower garden. "I

thought of this before, but it just didn't fit in with feet and yards."

We stared at the wood lilies and chicories and bouncing bets nodding in the dappled sunlight.

"Wait a minute!" McGurk strode over to the kitchen door, turned, and paced between there and the flowers. "Eight strides."

"Which is near enough to eight yards or twenty-four feet," said Brains. "Nowhere near fifteen *anything*."

"Of course not," said Wanda. "But now *you* try, G. B. And keep your strides normal."

Rather reluctantly, Brains did that. "Eleven," he said.

"Huh!" grunted McGurk. "Officer Yoshimura, you have a go."

Well, Mari came closer, with twelve paces, and that cheered him up a little. "It's still three short of fifteen, but—"

"Oh, come on, McGurk!" said Wanda. "It stands to reason. Someplace Mr. Smith was *used* to digging. Convenient for burying his stash. And these bouncing bets *clinch* it!"

"How, Officer Grieg?"

"Because they prefer *disturbed* ground. Like over at the burned-out motel. Just look how they flourish!"

That was enough for McGurk. "Good work, Officer Grieg! Let's get digging!"

"Be careful with the flowers, though," said Wanda.

But, carefully or clumsily, we failed to uncover any stash, despite the fact that we must have gone down two feet before hitting granite. And it was only when we were putting back the flowers that we made any further progress in our investigation.

For the second time, we were startled by a woman's voice asking almost the same question. *"Hey! What are you doing?"*

But this time it wasn't Ruth. This was an older person, in her late twenties, maybe early thirties, wearing a sloppy black sweater and baggy dark jeans. And yes, it had to be the woman Ruth had described. Her hair was very short and bristly, and this in itself made her look fearsome. But there was something about her face—a gray-white in contrast with those glaring eyes, heavily made-up with black eyeshadow—that had me feeling very uneasy. As if I'd seen her before. In a nightmare. Plus her dangling earrings—three-inch silvery chains with links from a heavier bicycle chain at the ends.

She was carrying one of those short spades that combat troops dig foxholes with.

And if her appearance stunned us into silence, just think what her next words did: "My father thinks the *world* of those flowers you've been messing with!"

·14·

The Jailhouse Logos

Your . . . *father?*" McGurk faltered.

"Yes," she replied. "Mr. William Smith."

Wanda cleared her throat. "Are—are you the person who's been hunting truffles?"

"Ha!" the woman cried. "*She* told you that, did she? Miss Snooty-britches with the horse? Well, that's what I told *her.* Actually, I was searching for wild orchids. A present for my dad. Something to add to his collection."

McGurk was now looking more like his usual businesslike self. "Does Mr. Byrne know you're here?"

"Who?"

"His—" I began.

"Be quiet, Officer Rockaway! . . . When did you last see your father, Ms.—uh—?"

"Smith, of course! Erika Smith. You can call me Erika, Red." She turned to me. "That's Erika with a *k*, Professor." Then she turned back to McGurk. "There's a famous painting called that. 'When Did You Last See Your Father?' Historical. Cavalier kids being interrogated by Roundhead law officers. Cops never change. What are *you* staring at, Professor? Wondering where I get all this stuff about famous paintings and Cavaliers? I read a lot. These last two years I've had nothing much else *to* do. Plus the fact that I am, after all, an author's daughter."

McGurk pounced on that. "Oh! So you *know*, then?"

"What? That Dad's really the great crime writer, Bill Legrand? Of *course* I do!" She jabbed the flower bed with her spade.

McGurk frowned. "So—when *was* the last time you saw him?"

Her face clouded. "Well . . . just over two years ago. We parted on kind of uneasy terms. But we've made up for it some since then. Through the mail."

"Did you know he disappeared?" McGurk asked. "About two months ago?"

"No. But I'm not surprised. That was around the time I heard he was in deep trouble."

McGurk looked up sharply. "What trouble?"

"Never you mind! I just heard a rumor on the grapevine, that's all."

"What grapevine?" Willie asked, wide-eyed.

"Never you mind *that*, either, Beaky! It was serious enough for me to make plans to come here and do what I could to help him."

She gave the soil another stab. I looked at the bouncing bets, then back at her.

"You . . . uh . . . took your time," McGurk was saying.

"Yes, Red. It wasn't that easy to arrange."

I was still staring at her, and now I was trying to imagine her with longer hair and a leaner, fitter face.

Then, *yes*, by golly!

"Ms. Smith," I said, "would you mind rolling up your sleeves?"

She looked at me long and hard. Then she grinned, said, "You're not as dumb as you look, Professor!" and did as I'd requested. First the left sleeve.

There were gasps from at least four different throats.

For sliding along that once nut-brown arm was the tattoo of a striking snake!

Then the right sleeve, uncovering . . . the tattoo of a zigzag bolt of lightning!

104

"Lady Thumb!" exclaimed Wanda.

"I'm going!" said Willie.

"Stay where you are, Officer Sandowsky!" commanded McGurk. Then, nodding his head slowly, he said one of those things he'd always wanted to say. "So—we meet again, ma'am!"

"Looks like it, Red," she murmured, giving him one of her old dazzling smiles. "I was wondering how long it would take *you* to recognize me."

Mari was looking bewildered. The case involving Lady Thumb had happened before she'd become a member of the Organization. We'd called it the Case of the Four Flying Fingers. This lady criminal had bribed four little kids to go around overturning people's garbage cans—using the kids to finger the houses where the people were on vacation and there was no one home to clear up the mess. *Those* houses she would then burgle. Which is why we called the kids the four fingers, and her Lady Thumb.

"Would you like to step inside, ma'am?" McGurk asked, nodding toward the cabin.

The woman shook her head, setting those weird earrings swinging. "No, thanks. Walls have ears." She flashed him another smile. "Didn't you know *that*, Red?" Then she became grave. "Anyway, if I were you, I'd watch my step. You could find you were dealing with

105

someone a heap more dangerous than any penny-ante lady burglar."

"You were dangerous enough yourself, ma'am," said McGurk. "The way you took off with us in your camper!"

"Yes, but I only did it to scare you," she said. "And I *did* intend to drop you off at the state line."

"Well, maybe you did. . . ."

"*Certainly* I did! But if we're up against the kind of people I think we are, you won't be so lucky."

"So . . . who *are* we up against?" Brains whispered.

"That's what I'm aiming to find out," she said. "This guy Byrne you mentioned—who's he?"

"Mr. Legrand's—your father's agent," said McGurk.

She nodded. "Ah, yes. I remember Dad mentioning him once. *He* should be okay. Anyone who gets ten percent of Bill Legrand's earnings sure has an interest in wanting him to stay alive!"

"You think someone might have—might be out to *kill* Mr. Smith?" said Willie.

"It wouldn't surprise me, Beaky."

"Why?" asked McGurk.

"Because, the way I heard it, Dad has something they badly want. In fact, all that's keeping him alive— if he still *is* alive—is the fact that they don't know where he's hidden it. Once he tells them that and they go and pick it up, he'll be a dead man."

Willie broke the shocked silence. "Will—will they be *torturing* him?"

"I doubt it. The trouble with torture is that the victim often dies before he spills the beans. My guess is they'll just be trying to wear him down gradually. Besides hoping he's left some clues for them to follow up themselves."

"What if they get what they want that way?"

"They'll kill him," said Erika Smith, snapping her fingers. "Just like that! So he won't be able to tell anyone whatever it was that he stumbled across."

"Wow!" murmured Wanda.

"Yeah," said the woman. "That'll be why Dad's been holding out so long." She now looked at McGurk with an urgent appeal in her eyes. "So if you've come up with any clues, Red, let's be hearing them."

McGurk was frowning. "How do we know you're not one of *them*? Someone they've hired to find out these clues?"

"Me? His own daughter?"

McGurk's eyes glittered. "How do we know you *are* his daughter?"

She took time out to think. "Hmm! That's a point." Then she looked up. "Tell you what—why don't you check with this Byrne guy, his agent?

He'll have heard Dad talk about me, if anyone has."

"Well . . ."

"Like for instance, these tattoos. They're what got him all steamed up two years ago. 'My only daughter!' he said. 'The only child of Bill Legrand! Turns up after all these years, and what does she have to show? Not only a petty criminal record but these jailhouse logos!' Which happened to be what he'd called tattoos in one of his Mike Parker books—*The Jailhouse Logo Slayings.* Where . . . where all four victims had tattoos they'd picked up in prison!"

She'd been crying as she told us this. She, Lady Thumb, the one we'd always thought of as probably our toughest, most hard-bitten adversary! Black streaks of eye shadow were running down her cheeks.

We didn't know where to look.

"I mean, I'd been promising him I'd live that record down, and—and I meant it. But after he saw the tattoos, he—he just didn't want to know!"

One slow tear had begun to roll down Wanda's left cheek. Mari looked very sad. Willie's sniffs sounded a tad wet. Brains was blinking and polishng his glasses. My own were getting kind of clouded up, too.

Only McGurk seemed unmoved. "So *then* what happened?"

"I stormed out, of course, vowing to pull off a *really*

criminal act and burgle all those houses in his own neighborhood and see how he liked *them* apples!"

"We'll check with Mr. Byrne," said McGurk, still looking suspicious.

"You do that!" she snarled. She turned and began to stalk out of the clearing.

"Then we'll be in touch?" McGurk called after her.

"Suit yourself!" she grated, without even turning her head.

"She seemed very upset!" said Mari.

McGurk blinked. "Oh, yeah, I was forgetting. Officer Yoshimura, do *you* think she was telling the truth?"

"Most of the time, yes, Chief McGurk."

"Congratulations, McGurk!" said Wanda. "You've just gone and offended our most valuable ally yet!"

"You can't be too careful!" he muttered. "Anyway, let's check it out with Mr. Byrne. . . . How long will it take you to fix this phone, Officer Bellingham?"

"Not long, with the right tools," said Brains.

"Well, right after lunch, make sure you bring them."

"Oh, yes," said Wanda. "I just remembered. On our way back here, why don't we stop by the museum, McGurk?"

"What for?"

"From what Erika says, it might not be a stash of

manuscripts we're looking for. It could be something much smaller."

"So?"

"So in the Felicity Snell book my mother borrowed from the library the other day—*Felicity Snell and the Pharaoh's Curse*—Felicity finds the murder weapon hidden inside a mummy case. In the museum next door to the library where she works. And it *is* our museum Bill Legrand had in mind in the book, I'm sure. There's even a statue of a fish in the pond outside. Just like ours. He even calls it Jaws the way some of the kids here do."

That "Jaws" bit grabbed McGurk, all right!

"Hey! It could be you're on to something there, Officer Grieg! First stop after lunch, men: the museum. We might have something to *tell* Mr. Byrne, not just *ask* him!"

·15·

More Clues

Joanne Cooper, the museum assistant, has always been very friendly toward us. But when we asked if we could take a peek inside the mummy case, she shook her head. "Sorry. It's against the rules."

McGurk swung around toward the case, propped up against the wall, behind a rope barrier. "But, Joanne—"

"And besides," said Joanne, "it couldn't be done. The case was sealed up years ago by the curator. And why? Because he'd gotten fed up with people wanting to take a peek inside. It's only a mummy *case*, anyway. There's no mummy inside."

But McGurk doesn't easily take no for an answer. "Sure. But how do we know someone hasn't broken the seal and opened it up *since*?"

"Well, considering it gets dusted regularly and none of the cleaners has reported any broken seal, I think we can assume that nothing like that *has* happened."

McGurk doesn't like to assume things, either. Not when we can check for ourselves.

"It won't take more than—"

"No!" said Joanne.

That was when Wanda decided to speak up. "The reason we're asking, Joanne, is this. . . ." Then she told our friend about the Felicity Snell book and the mummy case in which Felicity found the murder weapon, and how we believed that Bill Legrand had had this very museum in mind.

Joanne's eyes widened. "You mean *the* Bill Legrand? Here? In this town?"

"Yes," said Wanda. And she went on to explain how the description fit.

"So do you remember anyone else asking to take a peek?" said McGurk. "Like maybe Bill Legrand himself, researching for his book."

"Or trying to hide some—"

"Be quiet, Officer Sandowsky!"

112

Luckily, Joanne was too starry-eyed to take any notice of Willie's words.

"But I'd have remembered *that*! I mean, Bill *Legrand*!"

"Well . . . he's a very private person," said Wanda.

"And maybe he didn't ask permission," said McGurk. "Maybe he just snuck behind the rope and pried the seal open."

Joanne was so curious by now that she stepped behind the rope and took a look for herself. "No," she said. "Completely sealed. As always." She must have seen the disappointment in our eyes. "Hey! Cheer up! It didn't have to be sealed in *Mr. Legrand's* story. Writers are always doing that, you know. Changing the facts to suit their plots."

Then she sighed. "Bill Legrand, though! Visiting this museum! As soon as I take my break, I'm going to zip over to the library next door and see what they have about him in the reference room."

"Oh?" I said.

"Sure," she replied. "In one of those books that give you the biographies of different writers. I'm sure there's one that deals just with crime writers."

Well, that was enough for McGurk. Two minutes later, we were sitting at one of the big tables in the library's reference room, with the crime-writer volume in front of us.

"Hey, yes!" I said, opening it at the contents page. "Look! Number sixteen—Bill Legrand!"

As I flipped over the pages, revealing photographs of one author after another—some at work, some as kids, but mostly showing clearly what they looked like now—we really thought we'd be in business.

But no such luck. We'd forgotten what Mr. Byrne had told us. At the top of the page of pictures, it said, in heavy black type, this:

A notorious recluse, Mr. Legrand consistently refuses to publish a clear likeness of himself, even for his millions of devoted readers. Here is a selection of some of the pictures he has provided for the dust jackets of his numerous books over recent years.

And—well—I ask you—what help could the *following* possibly be?

#1. A picture captioned "The Author at Work," showing him typing at a desk with his back to the camera and a Mexican shawl hiding all but the top of his head. ("It might just as well be Clint Eastwood!" grumbled McGurk.)

#2. Captioned "Mr. Legrand Getting His Exercise"—not with his back to the camera this time, but wearing a ski mask, shoveling snow from around a small VW. ("Well, at least I can recognize the cabin in the background," murmured Wanda.)

#3. Another with the author-at-work caption; in close-up, too—but only of a pair of hands at the keyboard of a typewriter. ("That's the Remington portable," said Brains. "Sure!" said McGurk. "So what? I mean, just look at those fingers and thumbs! They could be *any-body's*. No rings, no marks, no moles, no tattoos—" "He doesn't like tattoos, Chief McGurk," Mari reminded him.)

#4. Another back view, labeled "Mr. Legrand Relaxes"—showing him out in some rocky wilderness, with his head, shoulders, and arms all hidden behind a *huge* backpack, and only a pair of legs and hiking boots visible. ("It's a good shot of those Douglas firs he's heading for," said Wanda. McGurk was too disgusted to comment. And only Willie reacted with any interest at the next and final picture.)

#5. Labeled "Mr. Legrand's Favorite Shot," plus this quotation: "As a writer, I think of myself as a fly on the wall, observing everything, hearing everything, noting everything, but keeping absolutely anonymous and insignificant myself—and therefore virtually invisible." And the picture? A close-up of a fly on a wall—what else? Here's a copy, just to show you what we were up against:

As I said, only Willie seemed impressed. "Hey!" he gasped.

"What?"

"I once saw a movie where this guy got changed into a fly. Maybe Mr. Smith—"

"Officer Sandowsky," said McGurk wearily, "shut up! Now!"

"But that could account for him disappearing—"

"I said *now*! Okay?"

116

"Well, at least Erika's story checks out," said Wanda.

"Huh?"

"Yes." Wanda pointed to something she'd been reading on the opposite page. "Here . . ."

Now that passage *was* worth copying. Here's what it said:

> A deep sadness in Mr. Legrand's life—and one that possibly accounts for his reclusive lifestyle—is the fact that when his wife divorced him over twenty years ago, she took with her their three-year-old daughter, Erika, whom he has never set eyes on since.

"Hey! When was this written?" said McGurk.

I turned to the copyright notice. "Three years ago."

"So there you are, McGurk," said Wanda. "I wouldn't mind betting that Erika saw this, and that's why she came to visit him two years ago. Reading that about her lonely dad's deep sadness. I know *I* would've."

"Yeah!" said McGurk. "Or maybe Lady Thumb read about all these best-selling books and figured how much she stood to gain by *pretending* to be his long-lost daughter."

Wanda flicked her hair back. "Sometimes I wonder about *you*, McGurk! You heard what Mari said. The poor woman was telling the *truth*."

117

"You can't be too careful, though," I said, backing McGurk up.

What was *really* eating me was the way Wanda had spotted that item before I, the word expert, had even gotten around to *reading* it.

"Anyway," I said, back on my mettle, "there's just one thing more *I'd* like to check out."

Mrs. Grunwald, who was on reference-room duty, frowned when I asked if there was a copy of Edgar Allan Poe's "The Philosophy of Composition."

"Isn't that rather an advanced subject even for *you,* Joseph?" she said.

I told her it was because we were interested in what Mr. Poe had to say about writing "The Raven"—and she laughed.

"Oh, *that*! Of course! That's a very famous essay of his. Various parts of it must have appeared in a *million* anthologies."

Then she went to the shelves, plucked out a book called *The Poet's Workshop,* glanced inside, and said, "Sure. Page sixty-seven."

I took it to the table, already opened.

"Officer Rockaway—"

I lifted my hand. Almost immediately, I'd found the bit I wanted. That was because someone had underlined it, very lightly, in pencil. Maybe a *little stub* of pencil at that—sharpened at both ends!

Here's a copy I made there and then:

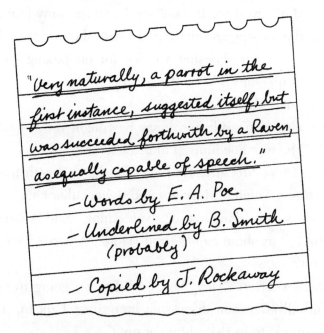

"*Very naturally, a parrot in the first instance, suggested itself, but was succeeded forthwith by a Raven, as equally capable of speech.*"

— Words by E. A. Poe

— Underlined by B. Smith
(probably)

— Copied by J. Rockaway

"There!" I said.

"*What* underlined?" said McGurk, peering at my notes, then back at the book.

"Get closer," I said. "It *is* very faint. Five or six lines from the bottom."

"Oh, yeah . . . anyway, what's so special about it?"

"Well, the tape," I said. "About the poem 'The Raven.'

And why Poe chose that bird instead of—uh—what were Bill Smith's exact words?" I closed my eyes, trying to recall precisely what he'd said.

But Mari saved me the bother. In an uncanny imitation of the missing author's taped voice, she murmured, " 'His reason for choosing a *raven* for his talking bird and not—uh—any other talking bird.'"

"So?" said McGurk.

"So why didn't Bill Smith say it straight out?" I argued. "The way Poe himself did: 'a *parrot*'?"

"Yes, Chief McGurk. And why did he end with that very strange laugh?" Mari imitated the peculiar chuckle.

"Like he was trying to tell us something," said Wanda.

"But tell us about *what*?" said Willie. "A parrot? Why a parrot?"

Brains snorted. "Hey, McGurk! Are we going to sit around all afternoon discussing literature? I mean, do you want me to fix that phone or not?"

McGurk gave a slight start. "Huh—sure, Officer Bellingham. You're right. We're wasting time. Let's go, men."

But there was now a *very* thoughtful gleam in his eyes.

·16·

And One Very Special Clue

Brains soon got that phone working again. He even fitted it with an extra amplifier so that we could all hear clearly what Mr. Byrne was saying.

"Bill himself didn't have any doubts about Erika. And when he'd gotten over the shock of that burglary rap, he gave her his full support. Paid for the best defense lawyers to make sure she got the lightest possible sentence. Wrote to her regularly and called her whenever he could. . . . Is anyone with you, McGurk?"

"Only my officers," said McGurk, glaring at Wanda, who'd just blurted out a heartfelt, "There! You see!"

Then Mr. Byrne continued. "In fact, Bill told me she was able to give him extra details about *you* guys. How

121

she called *you* Red, and another of you Beaky, and so on. Details he was able to use in *The Apostle Killings*."

McGurk suddenly became very beady-eyed. "Excuse me, sir, but you don't think he went over the top, do you? Supporting her?"

"How's that?"

"Well, like if she told him how she wouldn't have been arrested if it wasn't for us. Maybe they both planned to get back at us. To get us looking for the stash when all the time it's somewhere safe in a bank. Just to make fools of us."

"*Ha!*" Mr. Byrne's snort rattled the amplifier. "Fat chance! That would have meant fooling me, too, McGurk. And no one makes a sucker out of Sheldon Byrne!"

"Me either!" muttered McGurk, still beady-eyed.

"Anyway, forget Erika," said the agent. "She's probably getting worked up over nothing. Just like a woman. Bill's probably gone off on an extralong trip. But *my* problem is to supply the publishers with a new Felicity Snell book. So we've got to find that stash and dig one outa there. Any clues yet?"

"A few, sir. One especially. But it's too early yet to—"

"Well, move it, then!" said the agent. "It's getting urgent. As one principal to another, I'm counting on you, McGurk!"

Whereupon he hung up.

Wanda could hold back no longer. "Where does he think he gets off? 'Just like a woman!' How about just like a *principal*?"

"Huh?"

"Yes, McGurk! Completely heartless, just like *you*! What does *he* care about poor Erika—or her father? So long as we find the stash!"

"Hey!" said McGurk. "*I* care about Bill Smith and what's happened to him. I believe she was right about that. In fact, there's some evidence we knew already that supports it."

Willie, who'd been going cross-eyed watching a fly, suddenly blinked. "What evidence, McGurk?"

"The fact that he'd been going around gathering material for his book about crime and criminals in this area. I think he must have stumbled over something *really* big. Some piece of evidence that looked like blowing it sky high." McGurk looked very grave.

"What did you have in mind, McGurk?" I said. "When you told Mr. Byrne about one clue *especially*?"

"Oh, yes . . . *that*. Well, I haven't figured it out yet. Not completely. I'm hoping that by tomorrow—after I've drunk a lot of fresh orange juice—I'll be able to let you know where the stash is hidden."

Wanda groaned aloud.

"Do you have a problem with that, Officer Grieg?"

"Yes, McGurk! All you can think about is finding those—those precious manuscripts! When Mr. Smith's life is at stake and his daughter's going crazy with worry!"

"Not so fast!" said McGurk. "You're right there. Those manuscripts *are* precious. So the chances are that wherever he's stashed *them,* this terribly important evidence will be there, too!"

After that, even Wanda could raise no objection, and we all pedaled home hoping that he knew what he was doing and that the McGurk refrigerator wasn't low on oranges.

A couple of hours later, just before dinner, the doorbell rang at my house.

It was McGurk, looking anxious and kind of feverish. "That book. *Tales of Mystery and*—uh—"

"*Imagination?*"

"Yeah. Could I borrow it?"

"Sure," I said. "But is there anything *I* can tell you?"

"No. I need to read it myself." He must have seen my look of astonishment. "It's just another hunch I've had. . . . Come *on,* Officer Rockaway! It's urgent."

I thought maybe he was wanting to read "The Purloined Letter" and draw up a list of hiding places in furniture.

I mean, I was certain he didn't want to borrow the book for *pleasure* reading. Not McGurk! Not something by Edgar Allan Poe, without me at his elbow to explain the long words!

But I was wrong.

Boy, how *very* wrong I was!

·17·

McGurk Makes a
Book Report

When we went to the cabin the next morning, there was an enthusiastic gleam in McGurk's eyes.

"Officer Rockaway's right, men," he announced, placing the book on the table. "There's nothing to beat a good book."

We stared at him as if he'd flipped.

"I mean a video, okay." He sat down on the painted chair. "I guess it can be more—uh—*entertaining*. Like if they turn a story into a movie."

Willie had been staring at the fly, which was now sunning itself on the wall next to him. "Yeah! Like 'The Black Cat' thing and—"

"Sure, Officer Sandowsky," said McGurk. "Well, I don't know if they got around to making a movie out of 'The Gold-Bug' yet. And I have to admit that reading it is pretty tough going. But I'll tell you *this*. I'd never have been able to do with a movie what I did with the printed story itself last night."

"What's that, McGurk?" I asked.

"Concentrate on one special part. And go over it again and again until—"

"You could've if it had been on video," said Brains. "You could use the freeze-frame and—"

"And it *still* wouldn't have done what this book did!"

"Go on, McGurk," I said. "Did *what*? Yield up its hidden treasures?" I was thinking of its hidden treasures of *language*, of course.

"Right, Officer Rockaway!" he said. "Yield up its hidden treasure. I like that. Because it's sure yielded up *Bill Smith's* hidden treasure!"

We gaped at him.

"How . . . how do you work that out, McGurk?" Wanda asked in a hushed voice.

"Well, it didn't yield it up all *that* easily. But I suddenly had this feeling yesterday. After something you said in the library, Officer Rockaway." He paused. "I wondered if a door had featured in 'The Gold-Bug' story. And . . ."

I said earlier that never before had a bunch of kids listened so avidly to another kid's book report. I was referring to my own, of course. Well now, within days, that record was being broken. By McGurk, of all people!

"I found that door pretty early in the story, in fact. It wasn't much of a feature. It doesn't creak open at midnight to let in a homicidal prowler or anything."

"You sure it was the only mention?" I asked.

"You bet!" said McGurk. "The only one that mattered, anyway. I admit it's a long story, and I did get kinda drowsy toward the end. But luckily the door I'm talking about came in the first two pages, when I was fresh and alert."

"So?" said Wanda. "What did it tell you about the stash?"

"I'm coming to that." McGurk held up the expired membership card. "This says *G-B*, right? Meaning the story 'The Gold-Bug,' right? And the only other thing scribbled down here is *15 from door,* okay?"

I suddenly caught my breath as a picture flashed into my mind. Of me, yesterday, directing McGurk where to look for the underlined passage: *five or six lines from the bottom of the page.*

"So we naturally thought this meant a measurement," he was continuing. "Fifteen *feet,* fifteen *yards*—"

"Fifteen *meters,*" said Brains.

"Fifteen *paces,*" said Wanda.

"Right," said McGurk. "But we were *wrong*. He wasn't referring to length at all. Not that kind of length."

"What, then?" said Brains.

"Something to do with the position of the word *door*," said McGurk. "Inside the story. So—"

"Hey, yes!" I gasped. "Like—"

He waved me quiet. "So first I thought he meant words. Fifteen words after *door*. Or fifteen words before. But that only gave me—uh"—he glanced at the page—"*novelty* and—uh—*getting*."

"Well, what about—?"

"This is *my* report, Officer Rockaway. . . . So next I thought of lines. Fifteen lines after the line with *door* in it, and fifteen lines before. And that—"

"Objection, McGurk!"

He looked at me bleakly. "Well?"

"Lines wouldn't be much good as an accurate guide," I said. "They're like *paces* that vary according to the height of a person. Books like this come in all kinds of editions, and the lengths of lines vary according to the print size."

"Well, not being a *regular* word expert—who should have spotted this himself—*I* didn't know that," said McGurk. "So I went fifteen lines down and got—uh— 'it's so long since I saw you, and how could I foresee . . .' which didn't seem very helpful. And fifteen lines before, likewise. It says—'It is not improbable that the relatives of Legrand. . .'"

"Hey, *that* might be a pointer, McGurk!" said Wanda. "Now that we've met one of *our* Legrand's relatives."

"Yes, Chief McGurk," said Mari. "What does it say about them?"

McGurk sighed. "Simply that his relatives thought he was nuts. Uh—'unsettled in intellect' is what it says here. Now may I go on?"

"Yes, McGurk," I said. "How about paragraphs? They'd be the same whatever the edition, and—"

"Not so fast, Officer Rockaway! For one thing, the word *door* comes in only the fourth paragraph of the story. So that knocks out one-half of your suggestion right away. No. After words and lines, what comes next is—"

"Sentences!" I yelled.

"Right! Now you're thinking like a detective. Methodically."

"So what *are* these sentences, McGurk?" Wanda asked. "Fifteen before and fifteen after?"

"Well, in the fifteenth sentence after the one where *door* appears, we get this: 'It is of a brilliant gold color—about the size of a large hickory nut—with two jet-black spots near one extremity of the back, and another, somewhat longer, at the other.'" McGurk looked up. "That's the gold-bug itself he's describing."

130

"Maybe Bill Smith means for us to look out for one in here!" said Brains. "A goldsmith beetle. I checked in one of my insect books, and that's the real name."

"I wondered about that myself," said McGurk. "But there's no gold-bug in here. No dead body of one, like in the story. Not even a picture of one."

"We'd better check these *books* for a picture, all the same," said Wanda. "You never know—"

"Save it, Officer Grieg!" said McGurk. "Because now I'm going to read out the fifteenth sentence *before* this one."

It turned out to be so vital that later I photocopied it for our file, and here it is:

It is separated from the mainland by a scarcely perceptible creek, oozing its way through a wilderness of reeds and slime, a favorite resort of the marsh-hen.

There was an uneasy silence.

"What's the *it*, McGurk?" asked Willie. "The one that's separated from something."

"An island, Officer Sandowsky. Off the coast of South Carolina. But separated by a *creek*. Okay? A *creek* . . ."

131

He was looking around with an expression of unbelievably fiendish cunning on his face.

Wanda shrugged. "Well that's it, then. *We* can't go all the way to South Carolina to—"

"We don't *have* to, Officer Grieg! Think. What creek do we know around here? Going through reeds and slime? Huh?"

Brains jumped to his feet, one hand in the air. "*Brackman* Creek! Running through Brackman Swamp!"

"Why, yes!" said Wanda. "Where we—"

"Where we tracked down that bunch of *cat* thieves," said McGurk. "Who'd also stolen a *parrot*. Who'd *purloined* a parrot, in fact. The very case Mr. Smith came with Mark Westover to report on."

Mari was looking as excited as Brains. "The *tape*, Chief McGurk! The reading list! 'The Black *Cat*.' 'The *Purloined* Letter.' 'The Raven'—"

"That Poe had thought at first of making a *parrot*!" I chipped in.

McGurk nodded. "Bill Smith was spelling it out for us all the time, men."

I thought about Brackman Swamp. I mean, there was my own map of it in the files. We'd even shown it to Mark Westover that day, with Bill Smith looking over his shoulder. We'd had it at our fingertips all the time!

132

McGurk must have dipped into the files before coming, because he now produced that map. Here it is:

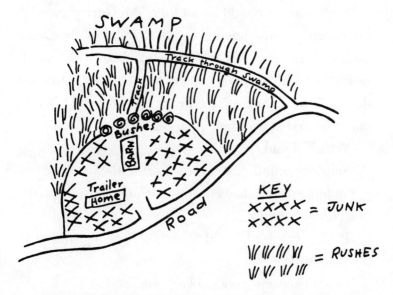

"There's even a door," said Willie. "The barn door."

"Two," said Wanda. "There's the trailer door as well."

"Which'll make it all the easier to pinpoint the stash," said Brains, his eyes shining with eagerness.

"If the trailer's still there," I said.

"Well, we'll soon find out." McGurk closed the book and got to his feet. "Where did you put your measuring string and stuff, Officer Bellingham?"

"It's back home, in the garage," said Brains.

A flash of annoyance crossed McGurk's face. "In your *garage*?"

"I took it back with me last night. I thought it wasn't much use anymore. Up here."

"Well, you were right about *that*!" McGurk glanced at his watch. "I was hoping to go straight to Brackman Swamp. Anyway, we'll just have to make a detour. It won't take long, and you can get some more birdseed at the same time. Also—" He broke off, his head tilted to one side. "What was that?"

"What?" I said.

"Scratchy sound. Just there—next to the window."

We looked. Wanda went to the window. I went to the front door. Nothing.

"Probably a bird," said Wanda. "Pecking around in the woodwork."

"*I* didn't see any woodpecker," said McGurk.

"No," said Wanda. "It was more likely a nuthatch. They can make a very loud noise for such small birds."

"Well, never mind," said McGurk. "Let's get going, men!"

I said nothing. But as Willie's fly brushed past my cheek and out through the open door, I was *thinking* a lot. Recalling what Erika Smith had said about walls having ears.

I was beginning to wonder if they wore long, scratchy earrings, too!

·18·

Pay Dirt

The junk yard at Brackman Swamp looked very different from how it did fourteen months ago. The trailer home was still there, but its windows and door were boarded up. The old barn looked pretty much the same, with its peeling red paint. But that, too, had a desolate air.

There was plenty of junk strewn around, though. Most of the big items had gone, but there were still piles of old tires and scattered bulging garbage bags, some of them with rusty engine parts spilling out.

Brains frowned. "How am I going to measure accurate semicircles with all that junk in the way? It'll be as bad as trying to do it among trees."

"Speaking of trees," said Wanda, "how come you didn't mark *that* one on your map, Joey?" She was pointing to a tall tree that stood at the edge of the yard, midway between the trailer and the barn. Cottony threads hung from the leaves and twigs.

"Because it didn't have anything to do with what we'd come for," I said.

"A very fine specimen of a swamp cottonwood," said Wanda.

"I don't remember those tires piled under it," said McGurk.

"No," said Wanda. "I think that's where Jeb Lee parked his car. In its shade."

"Yeah," grunted McGurk. "The car. I seem to remember *that*. Come on, men—give me a hand to clear these tires out of the way. Sling them over there and keep a clear track between the tree and the barn door. But not in front of the trailer, either, Officer Sandowsky!"

By now I was beginning to get his drift. So were some of the others. And very soon the ground there was completely clear. The coarse grass had continued to grow despite the tires, but the flattened stalks were straggly and white.

"Okay, Officer Bellingham," said McGurk, standing in

front of the tree trunk. "Just go to the barn door and measure the distance to here."

When Brains came back, keeping his string tight, he straightened up and said, "Just over fifteen feet. Say sixteen."

"Okay. Officer Yoshimura, you stand where the fifteen-foot mark is. . . . Now, Officer Bellingham, go measure from the *trailer* door."

This time, the yellow spot fell short of where Mari was standing, but only by about a foot.

"That's good enough for me!" said McGurk. "Look for signs of digging, men."

The ground had probably been quite hard in Jeb Lee's time, with parking his car there. But since then, the rains and snows must have worked on it to loosen it up. And—

"Hey!" yelled Brains. "How about if he . . . used this . . . as a marker?"

He was tugging at a flat, gray, irregular rock, only a few inches from where Mari had been standing. Not much bigger than a dinner plate, it looked too insignificant for a marker. But Brains kept on prying and tugging until—"There!" he said, freeing it and turning it over. "It—wow!"

It wasn't the centipede that went wriggling out of sight. Or the fat earthworm that slowly waved good-bye

137

before it, too, was out of sight. No. It was a beetle that we all gaped at now. One that wasn't going anyplace—being long dead.

Dead, but full of a kind of life as it glinted in the bright daylight.

"A *gold-bug*?" said Wanda.

"A goldsmith beetle!" said Brains, picking it up. "Yes. Look at its furry underside."

McGurk glowed with excitement. "Bill Smith must have put it there. This just *has* to be the spot, men! Get your trowels!"

We kept that dead beetle for our records. We even found a small glass case for it. It was a metallic yellowy green with—

But why not turn back and read Edgar Allan Poe's description. I mean, who am I, Joseph Jonathan Rockaway, to try and improve on *that*!

Anyway, none of us was interested in the beetle's actual description just then, as we began to dig. Especially when, about a foot down, we hit pay dirt.

"Easy, men!"

Black plastic gleamed up at us through crumbs of soil.

McGurk scraped carefully at the dirt.

"It's a bag," I said. "Folded over and over something pretty bulky."

"Yeah, to keep the damp from getting to it," said McGurk, hauling the bag free. "Look!" He unwound the plastic and revealed a briefcase of the old-fashioned kind: soft leather, with straps; more like a satchel.

"Locked?" asked Wanda.

"No," McGurk grunted, unfastening the straps and lifting the flap. "Why would he bother when it was going to be hidden so well?"

"*Another* plastic bag!" said Mari, as McGurk slid it out of the case. It, too, had been tightly wrapped around something bulky.

I was just beginning to wonder if it was going to be one of those joke parcels, with one thing wrapped inside another and on and on, when a bunch of school composition books suddenly slithered out onto the heap of soil.

"The manuscripts!" yelled Wanda as we picked them up. "Look! *Felicity Snell and the Secret of the Overdue Book!*" She was pointing to the handwritten title on the top one.

"Hey! *The Mincemeat Murders!*" said Brains, reading the one in his hand. "I bet this is a Mike Parker!"

Normally, I'd have been the first to grab a handful of these treasures, but right then I was more interested in something McGurk was holding.

"What's that, McGurk?" I could see that it was a

bulky sealed envelope, but he was busy squeezing it.

"Feels like there might be some tape cassettes inside," he murmured.

"Well, open it *up!*" urged Wanda.

"Uh-uh! It says—" Then he read out the inscription, holding it for us all to see.

```
NOT TO BE OPENED BY FINDER(S)

For the sole attention of
     Lieutenant Kaspar,
     West Milford P.D.

         URGENT!!
```

"Well done!"

We all spun around. For a second there, I thought it might have been Bill Smith himself, about to announce that this *had* been a game, after all.

But no. It was Mr. Craig Logan—stepping out through the door of the barn, dressed in his jogging gear. And despite the friendly smile as he came forward with his hand out, I suddenly began to wish we'd checked to see if that door was locked.

"What—what are you doing *here,* sir?" McGurk asked.

"I happened to be passing. One of my extended runs. May I see that?" The lawyer still had his hand out.

McGurk stepped back a pace. "It belongs to Mr. Smith."

"I'm not talking about the case and its contents." The man's smile was wearing thin. "He can have his manuscripts."

So he knows about *them*! I thought, as he continued, still advancing. "But there's something in that envelope that belongs to *me*! Hand it over!"

He wasn't smiling now.

"Sorry, sir!" said McGurk, taking another step back. "It says we're to give it to Lieutenant Kaspar, and—"

"And Lieutenant Kaspar would only pass it on to me," said Logan. "If he wished to keep his job, he would! So hand it over now and save—"

He'd been looking uglier and uglier, making me realize we were way out in the country, far from any possible help.

But Wanda, for one, wasn't taking any chances. At the word *save*, she yelled, "Here, McGurk!" and snatched the envelope from our leader's hands. Then, before anyone knew what she was doing, she'd stuffed it down the front of her shirt and was swarming up the trunk of that tree.

"You'll have to come and get it, Mr. Logan, if you want it!" she shouted down. "McGurk! You others! Go call the police—*now*!"

Well, the nearest house was more than a mile away. And, old as he was, Craig Logan, purple in the face and with glaring eyes, looked capable of accepting Wanda's challenge. In fact, he was already approaching the trunk, knees bent, ready to spring, when a voice rang out like a pistol shot.

"Don't bother, McGurk!"

Once again, we spun around.

It was Lieutenant Kaspar, just coming from behind the bushes. (The very bushes where we ourselves had hidden when we tracked down the cat thieves!) There were two more people with him: our old friend Patrolman Cassidy, and our new friend, Erika Smith.

"You can come down and give me that now, young lady," said the lieutenant. "And I'll take a chance on losing my job, counselor," he added, turning to Logan. "Thank you for confirming that there's something in that envelope that belongs to *you.* As I understand it, that something could put you away for at least seven to twelve years."

"Apart from what you get for kidnapping my father and falsely imprisoning him in your house!" said Erika, looking mad.

"What—what are you talking about, you—you *vagrant*?" stammered the lawyer.

"If I were you, Mr. Logan," said Lieutenant Kaspar, "I

would remain silent. She's talking about her father, William Smith, a.k.a. Legrand, who even as we speak"—he pulled out a two-way radio and extended its antenna—"is being freed. . . . " He pressed a switch. "Okay, Morelli?"

"Mission accomplished, sir," came the crackling reply.

"Unharmed, I hope?"

"So-so, sir; yeah," Morelli answered, bringing a smile to Erika's face.

The lieutenant nodded to his other companion. "Place him under arrest, Cassidy."

"And thank you all!" sang Erika, hugging McGurk as Mr. Cassidy put the cuffs on Craig Logan. "Thank you—oh, thank you—oh, thank you!" And with each "thank you" she planted a great big kiss on McGurk's already-burning cheeks.

"Yeah!" grunted Lieutenant Kaspar, sweeping us all with his icy blue eyes. "Thanks . . . I guess."

There were obviously no kisses coming from *him*!

· 19 ·

The Dull-Gray Bug

W e got more than kisses, though.

We got to meet and shake the hand of a very famous author. Bill Smith, a.k.a. Legrand, threw a party for us at his cabin, after he'd recovered from his ordeal in the Logan mansion.

Being a recluse, he might not have organized a very *special* party. But now that he had his daugther home to act as hostess, that party was something else: a glorious cookout in the clearing where we'd toiled so hard with our digging tools and measuring string.

There were juicy steaks, crisp Canadian bacon, four kinds of burgers, yummy corn-and-pepper fritters for vegetarians like Wanda and Lieutenant Kaspar, and french fries unlimited. There was even a bag of the best black sunflower seeds for the birds and chipmunks. Plus sandwiches galore, including submarines; seven kinds of doughnuts; a huge chocolate layer cake; and what seemed like a dozen varieties of soda.

McGurk, of course, stayed with fresh orange juice, saying he needed to keep a clear head because we had a few important loose ends to tie up.

The first concerned the scene at Brackman Swamp. "How did you know where we'd gone?" he asked Erika.

She was looking more like the Lady Thumb we'd first known. With a pair of light-blue designer jeans and matching shirt (long-sleeved), Erika seemed twenty pounds thinner. Even her face looked leaner and healthier without that ghastly white makeup. And although she hadn't had time yet to grow her hair back to its normal length, the blond wig helped a bunch.

She smiled radiantly at McGurk's question.

"Because I was listening outside the window when you gave your book report. And I don't apologize for eavesdropping. Not with my father's life on the line."

"And I don't blame you, Erika!" said Wanda.

"Okay," said McGurk. "But how did *Logan* know?"

"Because *he* was listening, too, Red."

"You mean outside the cabin, like you? Why didn't you warn us?"

"No! *Not* like me. Being the big-time crook he is, *he* used an electronic bug. Not a gold-bug—more a dull-gray bug. A small disc stuck to the underside of the table. I'm surprised you didn't spot it yourselves."

"Yeah!" growled McGurk, scowling at our science expert, who nearly choked on a mouthful of chocolate cake.

"But then, *I've* had more experience, I guess," said Erika. "Anyway, I noticed it the day I sprung the lock and broke in. Just before you guys first came here."

"That was *you*?" said McGurk.

"Yes. I was investigating my dad's disappearance, remember. But I was disturbed by the sound of Logan at the front door, and I slipped away. Then you came and—"

"But why didn't you warn us about the bug?"

"Because I was more concerned to find out who'd planted it. In fact, that was what made me first suspect Logan. I knew whoever planted it had to be working out of a vehicle parked nearby—on account of the range of the device. But there *were* no parked vehicles. So that left the nearest house. Logan's."

After that, she'd concentrated on the Logan mansion. Casing it like only an ex-burglar knew how. Getting friendly with one of the maids. Hearing from her that two new people had been hired recently. Paramedics in

146

hospital whites—but ugly-looking characters who'd have nothing to do with the regular staff. The story was that they'd come to look after a Logan relative who needed twenty-four-hour-a-day care, with no one else allowed in that wing of the mansion. "Not even Miss Ruth," the maid had added.

"Which is what convinced me that the 'relative' was really Dad, being held prisoner," said Erika. "And I was right. As soon as Logan heard over the bug that you'd discovered where the stash was located, he made a bee-line for Brackman Swamp. I spotted him just as I was about to make my own beeline there. I'd parked my camper along the Brackman Station road, and when I saw him leap out of the woods just ahead and run off as if his life depended on it—"

She looked around at us and shrugged.

"Well, then I thought I'd better break my golden rule and bring in the police. Pronto. I mean, there was no telling what a guy like that might do if he saw you'd un-earthed the evidence that could ruin him."

McGurk was looking very downcast at this point. When it comes to bringing in the police, he—and *only* he—likes to be the one to do it.

Erika laughed. "Cheer up, Red! This is still your col-lar. If it hadn't been for you and your buddies, Logan would never have been drawn into the open like that."

"Very true!" said Bill Smith, who'd come across to join us. "The evidence I'd found only *pointed toward* Logan's being the mastermind behind a statewide property fraud. It would still have needed a lot of checking and cross-checking before anyone could make it stick."

"But it was strong enough to have him scared, sir?" said McGurk.

"You bet! At first, back in April, I wondered if my informant was putting me on, fingering someone as highly respected as Craig Logan, Esquire. But then I heard a week or so later that this informant had met with a mysterious fatal accident. And I became even more uneasy when Logan stopped by for a neighborly chat and asked me about my work, kind of casually—"

"Did he know you were Bill Legrand, sir?" I asked.

"If he didn't, he soon got to know! But all he said at first was, 'I hear you're thinking of writing a book, Mr. Smith.' I denied it, of course. I always do if anyone seems to be getting close to discovering I'm Bill Legrand. But it set the alarm bells ringing, so I decided to take a few precautions."

"Like hiding the evidence?" said Wanda.

"Yes. Just in case." Mr. Smith laughed. "Like literally just in case—the briefcase I keep my manuscripts in. Normally, I don't bother to bury them. I just keep them by me, ready to grab if there should be a fire." He laughed again. "But I knew that if anything happened to me, Shelley here would be desperate to find them."

"You can say that again!" said Mr. Byrne, dabbing at a spot of sauce on his fine business suit.

"So, knowing that," said Bill Smith, "I deliberately laid a trail that would involve you guys. I hid the stash plus the envelope in a secluded place that was very special to you all. With clues that only you would be able to figure out correctly."

"But how did you know Mr. Byrne would come to us, sir?" asked McGurk. "And not some regular New York detective?"

"Because, like I told you," said Sheldon Byrne, "I knew Bill wouldn't want any publicity about his disappearance."

"Exactly!" said the famous author. "Even less so with evidence as hot as this involved. And anyway, I made sure of it by labeling that reading-list tape 'Notes for the McGurk Organization.'"

"Gee!" McGurk beamed around. "And we *did* figure those clues out, men!"

"Yes," said Mr. Smith. "I counted on you, and you didn't let me down. . . . Let me help you to some more juice, McGurk. You others, top up your drinks. I'd like to propose a toast to the McGurk Organization's seven members."

"*Seven*, sir?" said McGurk. "But—"

"Yes. To the McGurk Organization, ladies and gentle-men, and its seventh member—Edgar Allan Poe!"

Well, everyone drank to that, all right!

Even Lieutenant Kaspar raised his glass of celery juice and took a thin sip.

And that's about it. Except for the three new labels at the bottom of the McGurk Organization sign:

```
ABSENT AUTHORS
MADE PRESENT.
```

```
CODED CLUES COLLECTED,
CAREFULLY CONSIDERED
- AND CRACKED
```

Oh, yes. And one other thing.

Since Erika Smith's revelations about the electronic bug, McGurk has nearly driven us mad with his new training sessions. Four of them in less than two weeks! He's painted a thumbtack dull gray, which he hides somewhere in our HQ. Then the jerk has us crawling and climbing all over the place until we find it.

When I protested that this was a cruel and unusual punishment for our oversight, he said, "Punishment nothing, Officer Rockaway! It's a wise and proper precaution. You know the saying, 'Once bitten, twice shy.' Well that goes for being bitten by an *electronic* bug!"

Then he scowled and spoke tough, the way Lieutenant Carmichael does on television: "And that just ain't never gonna happen again to *this* Organization!"

I sighed. "I guess you're right, McGurk. The grammar stinks, but there's nothing wrong with your thinking!"